SHADOWS IN THE SANDS

SHADOWS IN THE STARS
BOOK 4

T.W.M. ASHFORD

DARK STAR PANORAMA

Dark Star Panorama is the shared universe of sci-fi stories in which *Shadows in the Stars* takes place. Other series include *Final Dawn, Kapamentis Crime* and *War for New Terra*.

To hear about new releases and receive exclusive free content, sign up for T.W.M. Ashford's mailing list at the website below.

www.twmashford.com

BOOKS IN THE "DARK STAR PANORAMA" UNIVERSE

Final Dawn Series

- The Final Dawn
- Thief of Stars
- A Dark Horizon
- The New World
- The Tin Soldiers
- Ghost of the Father
- The Stellar Abyss
- The Edge of Night
- The Fatal Dark

War for New Terra Series

- Sigma
- Iron Nest
- Royal Blood

Shadows in the Stars Series

- Shadows in the Stars
- Shadows in the Snow
- Shadows in the Stone
- Shadows in the Sands
- Shadows in the Salvage
- Shadows in the Storm

Kapamentis Crime Series

- A Cut Below
- Cut to the Bone
- Cut and Shut
- The Final Cut

Standalone Novels

- Saturnalia

SELECT NON-DSP TITLES

- Checking Out (Box Set)
- Blackwater (Box Set)
- The Portrait Lingers Like a Whisper
- Gerald Oddman

SHADOWS IN THE SANDS

Cerulean waves lapped gently against a shore of coral pink sand. Smooth-beaked pterosaurs the size of house cats glided through a sun-stained sky and eight-legged crustaceans scuttled through the frothy surf.

Four ex-pirates lay on padded sun loungers under a leafy cabana, sipping on exotic cocktails and enjoying doing absolutely nothing.

An ethereal puff-ball of a waiter floated past them holding a tray of twisty glass beverages. Gecki plucked a fresh drink at random and flashed the attendant a sharp-toothed grin. A shirtless Sheni leaned across from his adjacent lounger and nudged her with his elbow.

"Ain't this the life? Unlimited grub. Salty sea breeze. Rum punch, light on the punch. Don't see why we can't do this forever."

"Hepatic encephalopathy," Alan gurgled, slurping kwagua juice through a curly straw.

For years the crew of the *Silver Hart* had struggled to make ends meet. Always searching for the next big gig, scrimping and scraping, agreeing to whatever dangerous jobs they could just to keep themselves fed another half-cycle. And then they'd discovered the lost Sword of Bokata, a legendary blade with supernatural properties (which after careful study had turned out to just be the effect of a mind-warping fungus infused into the metal). It sold at auction for twelve point four million credits, minus a small commission fee. Now the four of them were filthy rich, and they didn't even know how to spend it.

A couple of weeks at a fancy Queflian resort struck them as a good way to start.

Gecki, the ship's reptilian captain, pulled her lounger out of the cabana's shade so she could bask in the sun. Sheni, who was human and hadn't been able to find any information on the planet's level of ultraviolet rays, stuck to the shade. Xotl, the five-armed purple starfish who piloted the *Silver Hart*, sat up in a curled position beside him drinking through a straw that was fed delicately through an intake filter in their transparent enviro-suit. And Alan, the small green jellybean with eyes like rotating dinner plates, now stood half-buried in the sand, having spent the past thirty minutes bobbing around in the ocean like a buoy.

Behind them, right at the top of the beach, rose the cream-coloured dome of the Nova Elysia luxury resort. Over one hundred rooms of pink-trimmed opulence and elegance. Half a dozen restaurants that would be the envy of anyone living in the Platinum neighbourhood of humanity's Ark ships, and the same number again of fancy bars stacked high with spirits suitable for a thousand different metabo-lisms. A full spa complete with mud baths and freshwater pools for the resort's more aquatic clientele. A high-tech virtual reality projection theatre capable of entertaining sixty-four users at a time. Weird birds with aggressively large plumage that seemed to wander the halls without inter-ference.

Further back, the spaceport in which the *Silver Hart* was parked was totally obscured by dense walls of tropical trees. While ahead, and all they could see from their spot on the otherwise deserted shoreline, was an endless stretch of crystal ocean meeting indigo and apricot sky, captured in a bay flanked by grassy red sandstone cliffs whose rocks crept past the waves in stacks, stumps and spits.

"I was disappointed not to join you at the auction," Xotl said through the clacking beak in the central disc of their body. They'd been recovering from a nasty gunshot wound in a hyperbaric chamber at the time. "But this experience more than makes up for it. Far more sanitary than that Corpse & Casket bar you like to frequent, too."

"How are those coconut spritzes treating you?" Sheni asked, leaning back and lacing his fingers together behind his head.

"They are treating me rather well, thank you for asking," the Xocha replied. "I've never really understood the appeal of alcohol, what with my species being unable to metabolise the stuff, but I must admit the pleasantly strange effect these liquified drupes have on me is quite appealing. No wonder you buy so many beers."

"I'm not sure an allergic reaction is quite the same thing as getting drunk," Gecki snarled with her eyes shut, "but I'm glad you're having fun."

"Oh, look," said Sheni, shielding his eyes from the sun. "Here comes trouble."

"Has Alan dragged a fish out of the sea again?" Gecki rasped. "Make him throw it back unless he intends to eat it."

"Nah, it's Mr. Zelewyn, the hotel manager. He's heading right for us."

"Gah, what does he want now?" She sat upright. "Haven't we given him enough credits already?"

"I imagine that's why he's paying us so much attention..."

Mr. Zelewyn was a Qualian, the species indigenous to Queflia, and practically the personification of every trait his kind was said to possess. Elegantly graceful, sharply intelligent and incessantly polite, his curved, waxy-smooth form swept toward their cabana on a pair of long-toed prehensile feet that scarcely seemed to touch the sand.

"Greetings," he said in a light, breathy voice that made Sheni think of sunlight refracting off a wine glass. "Making use of your unlimited libation privileges, I see. Very good. I trust you are all having a pleasant morning?"

"Indeed we are," Sheni replied, flashing Mr. Zelewyn a toothy grin. "Though I didn't realise it was that early. I guess we're still getting adjusted to the planet's rotation."

"Morning, evening – what's the difference?" Gecki reclined on her lounger and closed her eyes again. "It's the same angle of sun, ain't it?"

"How very astute of you, Ms. Gecki." The Qualian hotel manager took care to ensure he didn't cast a shadow over his sunbathing guest. The copper beads adorning his question-mark shaped torso jingled pleasantly. "As you know, the team here at Nova Elysia are available thirty-two hours a day to accommodate any needs you might have, no matter how species-specific. Speaking of which – no adverse reactions to those beverages, I hope, Mixter Xotl?"

"None at all," Xotl replied, flapping an arm. "Thank you so much. I never would have thought of drinking copra for the inebriating qualities of its foreign proteins."

"I shall pass your thanks on to our bartenders. They will be pleased."

"I'm sorry," Gecki rasped impatiently, opening her one good eye to glare at Mr. Zelewyn. "Is there a reason you came all the way down the beach to see us? I'm sure there's lots you need to be doing in a resort this big."

"You are quite right, Ms. Gecki, and I apologise if my presence has disturbed your peace in any manner." Sheni found it impossible to tell if a Qualian was smiling, or even if they were looking at him sometimes. Without visible eyes or an expressive mouth their heads were basically just arching stumps of smooth flesh, and the emotional inflections of their voice were far too subtle for a human to pick up. "I simply came to personally inform you of the entertainment options available to you this rotation. Oculus Lyloth are performing in the Centauri Theatre this evening. Limited matinee slots for tomorrow afternoon are also available."

"Is that an Oortilian band?" Gecki waved the offer away. "Nah. Can't stand their voices. Sounds like someone running their claw around the rim of a glass."

"You are quite right, Ms. Gecki. Then may I perhaps interest you in an ocean excursion? Our yacht is due to set sail for the outer basin later today. The *Mesonychoteuthis exocoetus* display really isn't to be missed."

"Oh, that sounds cool." Sheni sat up and nodded at Xotl, who flexed their arms agreeably. "Those are the flying squids, right? What do you say, Gecki? Want to check them out?"

Gecki growled deep in her throat.

"I'd rather bask in the sun."

"You can bask in the sun on a boat, you know."

Gecki appeared to mull this over.

"Yeah, fine. So long as the boat's got booze, I'm in."

"Splendid," Mr. Zelewyn exclaimed. "I shall reserve

tickets for the four of you. You may head over to the dock and enjoy the vessel's amenities whenever you're ready."

"Thanks, man." Sheni took another swig of his fruity drink. "You know, this place you've got here. It's really something."

"You are most welcome, Mr. Dupont." Mr. Zelewyn remained in front of their cabana, only now he angled his featureless head to face the bay beyond the shore. "And most correct, as well. Nova Elysia is one of the finest resorts in all of Queflia. But what I wouldn't do to install an observation tower to the north there, build a seafood restaurant overlooking the southern spit…"

The hotel manager collected himself and bowed to his esteemed guests.

"Apologies for my intrusion. I get carried away with myself sometimes. Please, enjoy your stay."

Mr. Zelewyn glissaded across the sands back in the direction of the hotel's grand dome. Gecki peeled open an eye to watch him go.

"Strange guy."

"Nah, he's all right. He's just a Qualian, that's all."

"Yeah, but all Qualians are odd. It's the way they're shaped. Feels like I'm being followed around by a query."

"That's speciesist, Gecki," Xotl spluttered.

"Ah, sue me. I'm rich enough to have unpleasant views."

They lay back and listened to the soothing sound of waves crashing. One of the small pterosaurs gliding above the shore shot down and plucked a fish from the water with its long, pointed beak.

"How many credits do we have left, anyway?" Sheni asked.

"A lot," Gecki rasped. "Haven't even broken the twelve million credit mark. The auction cut, the fee for this place, the cost of upgrading our ship and enviro-suits... Yeah, I'd say we're sitting at about twelve million credits, give or take."

"Man. Feels like we could just do this forever, you know?"

"I'm not sure it's a wise investment to spend that many credits on sun and sand," Xotl spluttered in between sips of coconut spritz.

"Well, we wouldn't spend all of it *here*," Sheni replied. "Kapamentis clubs, luxury starliners – there's a whole galaxy of grandeur to enjoy."

"And then what?" Gecki rasped. "What will we do when the credits run out?"

Alan made a slurping, sucking noise through his straw as he reached the end of his drink, a noise that only stopped when Sheni leaned forwards and took the glass away.

"It'll be a long time before we get through twelve million credits," he said, "even in places like this. But I guess I see what you mean. You thinking we should invest it, or something?"

"Or something, yeah. We could buy more ships."

"Like a fleet?"

"Yeah."

"Ships depreciate in value," Xotl interjected. "That would be a bad investment unless you used those ships to generate additional wealth somehow. Property would be wiser."

"A penthouse on Kapamentis would be freakin' awesome," Sheni added.

"If either of you believe twelve million credits will get you anything better than a cruddy tower apartment on that city-planet," Gecki snarled, "you'd better think again. But maybe a condo in the outer systems, or whatever. What else do rich people spend their money on?"

"Legendary swords with pseudo-magical properties?" Sheni suggested.

"Digital artwork?" was Xotl's input.

"Taffeite ovum," Alan giggled.

"Great ideas, everyone. Real lateral thinking." Gecki rolled her eye. "Eh, there ain't no rush. It's just nice to *not* have to worry about credits for once."

Sheni shook his drink. It was empty. Even the ice had melted. He grudgingly scooted off his lounger.

"I'm gonna get a refill, if anyone wants anything." He gave Gecki a prod on his way out of the cabana. "You know, there *was* something every super-rich socialite back on Earth ended up buying sooner or later."

"Yeah?" Gecki rasped distantly as she slipped into a hot nap. "And what's that?"

Sheni pointed down the shoreline to the dock.

"A really big boat."

CHAPTER
TWO

Qualians aren't anywhere near as sentimental toward inanimate objects as humans can sometimes be, and so it was that the yacht tethered to Nova Elysia's dock had not been given a name, female-leaning or otherwise. Had it been moored in an Earth or New Terran port, Sheni reckoned it would have had something trite like *Diamond Aurora* written in cursive down its side.

Personally, he would have called it *Buoyoncé*.

It sure was glorious. Not quite a superyacht but still requiring a few crew members to operate at any given time, it measured thirty-five metres in length and boasted a dining room (only serving pre-prepared dishes, however), an automated massage parlour with settings for mammals, insectoids and reptilians (sorry, Xotl), and an open-top observation deck. No swimming pool, holo-deck or landing pad, though. Such extravagance is probably difficult to justify in a resort's yearly budget, Sheni reckoned, when one already has multiple iterations of each on land only a few miles away. A pair of long, white hydrofoils stuck out to either side of the ship. Its bow curved up and out of the water like a forward-facing rhinoceros horn.

"Reckon we could stick a set of thrusters on it and turn it spaceworthy?" Sheni said, playfully elbowing Gecki in the ribs.

"Pah! Now there's an idea..."

The four crew members of the *Silver Hart* strolled down the polyethylene pier together, Xotl keeping pace by rotating from one pair of arms to another in a cartwheeling motion. A watercraft and submersible rental facility stood nearby, half built in the water, its bay-facing wall missing so vessels could come and go. Two Oortilians skipped over waves on water scooters a couple of hundred metres in the distance. A few other guests from the hotel were already on board the yacht, leaning over the railings of its top deck with drinks and snacks in their hands. Beside the short gangway at the end of the dock was a well-fed Garnidian. Their species normally struggled to stay healthy outside of their home system, but Sheni supposed this one had easy access to the best nutritionists. They broke into a friendly smile as if they were seeing old friends for the first time in years.

"Mr. Dupont, Ms. Gecki, Mixter Xotl and, erm..." They glanced down at the gormless green creature standing before them and then furrowed their brow as they scanned the list of names on their data pad. "Ah, yes – Mr. Alan. Welcome aboard. Please make yourselves comfortable."

"Don't mind if I do," Gecki said, snatching a drink from the tray proffered to them at the top of the ramp.

It was at this moment that Sheni first suspected he might never fit in with this crowd, regardless of how many credits lined his pockets. Half of the other passengers mingling amongst the velvet drapes and marble busts and crystal chandeliers had probably been born rich, while the rest likely worked their arses off until they were the heads of corporate empires (probably decapitating a few heads on their way up, too). Whereas deep down – hell, barely a layer of skin beneath the surface if Sheni were honest with himself – he was nothing but a lousy space-pirate who got lucky selling an old sword. And the other guests, with their curious glances and upturned snouts – Sheni reckoned they could smell the stink of spacer on him.

But screw them, right? He had an equal share of twelve million credits to his name. Why in the galaxy would he give two craps what a bunch of posh toffs thought of him?

He relieved the smiling attendant of their tastiest-looking drink and followed the rest of his crewmates down the semi-exposed hallway running the length of the yacht's exterior. Sheni winced as he took a sip. The drink was sharp, but in a good way. Some kind of Drygg vodka, maybe, with a kwagua juice mixer. That suited him fine. Good for getting drunk, and excellent for curing tomorrow's hangover, too.

A couple of extravagantly robed Mansa visibly recoiled as they spotted Gecki stomping up the steps toward the observation deck at the front of the yacht. Sheni felt a hot rage wash over him and had to keep from tightening his hand into a fist. These fancy glasses looked terribly fragile, and bleeding all over the floor would only add to his group's image as undeserving barbarians. Fortunately, Gecki didn't seem to notice the way they'd looked at her. If she had, it would be somebody else staining the seagrass carpets.

"Is anyone sitting there?" she rasped, reaching the top of the steps and pointing a claw at one of the reclining chairs positioned carefully around the deck. "No? Good. I will, then. Can someone get me a refill?"

For the second time in as many minutes, Sheni had a revelation: out of the four crew members of the *Silver Hart*, he was the only one wearing clothes. (And no, Xotl's transparent enviro-suit didn't count.) That in itself wasn't a problem – many species had evolved without the shame of nakedness, and the rest of the galaxy's citizens had long since gotten used to it. There wasn't exactly much to see on a starfish, anyway. But usually those with wealth adorned themselves with gowns and jewellery and trinkets to show off just how rich they were. Gecki wasn't even wearing her little spacer jacket. The four of them looked like they'd wandered in off the street.

Still, they hadn't, and Sheni would be damned if he didn't enjoy what they'd paid for.

Another of the ship's attendants provided Gecki with a fresh libation just as Sheni joined her by the recliners. He looked around for Alan and discovered him climbing the comm mast. He decided to pretend this wasn't happening. Better not to draw attention to him.

"You were right," Gecki rasped as he sat down. "This is much better than lounging on the beach. We're *way* closer to the bar."

"Oh, yes, coz *that's* why we're on the boat. You know, if all you wanted was to get drunk, we could have just gone to the Corpse & Casket. The beers are cheaper."

"They're weaker, too. And there ain't no sun at the Corpse. Barely a heater. And the air only tastes salty there coz of all the sweat."

"Yeah, I suppose that's true. But can you at least *try* to enjoy the flying squid, yeah? It's a once in a lifetime experience."

Gecki snorted through her slitted nostrils.

"It ain't once in a lifetime if you can come back and see them again tomorrow. But fine, sure, whatever. I'm sure the view will be *spectacular*."

"*I'm* looking forward to it, Sheni," said Xotl, propped up on the table beside them. They had another coconut spritz in their curled arm. "I believe it's important for me to sample as many unique experiences as possible in the remaining years I have left."

Sheni exhaled deeply, shook his head, and took another sip of his drink.

"All right, Xotl. Keep it light, yeah?"

The yacht set off from the dock a few minutes later, slowly at first, quickly building speed, then gliding silently over the water on its twin hydrofoils at a rate of thirty knots. The brisk sea air whipped against Sheni's cheeks. The assorted guests on the top deck clasped the railings and tittered with amusement. Even Gecki let out a surprised laugh. You can travel the stars faster than the speed of light and it still won't prepare you for the thrill of cutting through the open seas.

Sheni sniggered quietly to himself. This was only the second time he'd ever been on a boat. And the first had just been a slow ferry across the Seine. Barely counted. Some kind of pirate he'd turned out to be...

Well, he wasn't a pirate anymore.

Which begged the question: what *was* he?

The yacht slowed to a stop just outside of the bay, only a mile or so from where they set off, where the seabed grew much deeper. The rest of the coastline past the basin was just as beautiful – sandy shores of pink, luscious green jungle canopies, the occasional blemish of brilliant white to signify a secluded condo. Wherever Sheni looked, the ocean went on forever. Small islands balanced on the horizon flickered in a heat haze.

More drinks were brought out. Nibbles, too – nuts and molluscs and weird salty wafers that Sheni found incredibly moreish. The last few guests who'd stayed downstairs to hobnob with one another climbed the steps to join in.

"Esteemed guests," announced the Garnidian attendant who'd checked them onto the boat. "Thank you for joining us today. Please, help yourselves to the drinks and snacks. If you'll permit me to—"

"Where are the squid?" one of the Mansa shouted from near the back of the gathered crowd. Their jowls wobbled cantankerously. "Isn't that what we came to see?"

"You did indeed," the attendant replied. Sheni could tell they didn't possess quite the same level of stoic patience as Mr. Zelewyn. "But as I was just saying, the *Mesonychoteuthis exocoetus* are creatures of the wild and therefore not bound to any schedule. Technically speaking, there's no guarantee we'll even catch a glimpse of them today. However," they hurriedly added, sensing their audience's disapproval, "their flourish of activity over the past quarter-cycle suggests we *should* witness their display within the next hour or two. In the meantime, please allow me to provide some context for our visit."

Sheni leaned back and popped a couple of salty crackers into his mouth. Unlike some of the other guests, he was used to not having things appear at the click of a finger. As far as he was concerned, a few hours spent chilling on a boat waiting for a bunch of jumping cephalopods sounded pretty freakin' neat.

"Although we are permitted to sail upon the surface outside of the bay," the Garnidian continued, "these waters are actually considered the territory of a Plillup tribe who crashed here almost eight hundred years ago after their colony ship's drive core malfunctioned. Although the settlement was considered illegal at the time, the subaquatic town of Porto Kumasa is now protected under both Queflian and Ministerial law alike."

"If someone pulled that kind of stunt in *my* backyard," an Oortilian guest whispered to a neighbouring Krolak, "they'd be dust before they could erect so much as a mud hut."

Sheni shook his head. Even Gecki had the decency to roll her eye in exasperation.

"Though the residents of Porto Kumasa are extremely reclusive," the attendant said, ignoring their guests as they recited what was probably a memorised script, "it is believed that they've developed a special, perhaps even symbiotic relationship with the squid we've come here to see today, breeding and training them the way some species raise livestock. If you do see a Plillup along the far shores of the resort, by the way," they added, "I would advise you not to approach them. They're normally quite harmless, but isolation has made them somewhat wary of outsiders. As for their squid, well, they're a rather showy bunch while in—"

"Look," the Krolak guest grunted, pointing past the front of the boat. "There's one now!"

Everybody sat up in their chairs or ran to the front of the deck for a better look. Suspended above the water was an enormous squid, perhaps twenty metres in length from mantle to tentacle. Its glistening skin was a reflective greeny-blue colour. It appeared almost to fly as its nickname suggested, coasting on its splendid pectoral fins for a few seconds before plunging back down beneath the waves.

"Oh," the posh Oortilian muttered, tilting his head. "Was that it?"

The slender blue alien stumbled backward and spilled his drink as the yacht rocked to one side. The assorted guests cooed and laughed as half a dozen more flying squid burst from the ocean around them mantle-first, their long arms and tentacles draping behind them like fleshy ship rigging, blotting out the sun and raining seawater onto the deck. They coasted together, sparkling like stars as they defied gravity for but a moment, and then crashed down to rock the boat once more. The curved crests belonging to another pack of squid broke the surface seventy or eighty metres further ahead.

"I think I saw a Plillup riding one of them," Sheni said to Gecki in disbelief. Both had risen from their reclining chairs. She was picking at her teeth in amusement. Xotl had cartwheeled toward the front of the deck.

"You wouldn't be the first," replied the Garnidian attendant beside them. "Incredible, isn't it? If only we could ask them to teach us. It would make for a fantastic excursion. Can I fetch you another drink, sir?"

"No, but perhaps you can tell me who *they* are..."

Three small, rickety ships roared across the sea toward the squid. Each was propelled by a harsh, fiery thruster that turned their wake to steam. Judging by their angle of approach, it looked like they originated from further down the coast, or perhaps one of the larger islands to the south.

"I'm guessing they're not part of the tour?" Sheni asked.

"No," the attendant said, hurriedly rushing off down the steps. "No, they most certainly are not."

Sheni and Gecki pushed forward through the crowd to where Xotl stood half-coiled around a railing. A few of the other guests had started expressing their concern, too. Two of the ships continued on their original trajectory toward the giant cephalopods, but the third had splintered off and was now headed toward their luxury yacht at breakneck pace.

"This does not look promising," Xotl said morosely.

"Yeah, something tells me they ain't here to marvel at the majesty of nature," Gecki snarled.

The two ships still heading for the squid slowed, throwing up walls of seawater around them as their thrusters swivelled downward to keep them airborne. If Sheni squinted he could make out small figures rushing about on each ship's upper deck. The squid must have sensed danger, or at least been put off by all the disturbed water, because their pack – no longer leaping through the air – turned as one in a northerly direction.

A harpoon shot out from the bow of each ship. One plunged deep into the water and the chain tethering it to the ship grew slack. A miss. But the other pierced the side of one squid's mantle and burst out the other. Sheni could see the violent gush of blood from all the way back on the yacht.

The assorted guests around him gasped and clasped their chests in shock. This was hardly the view they'd paid for.

"Poachers," Gecki snarled, baring her teeth. "The worst."

"Somebody has to do something," Sheni snapped. "Who do we call on Queflia? The Ministry?"

"Wouldn't make any difference. By the time law enforcement gets here, those poachers will be long gone. Besides, we've got bigger problems of our own to worry about."

She pointed a claw past the bow of the yacht. The third poacher ship sprayed the lower decks with hot mist as it drew level with them. No harpoons this time. They were looking to board.

Sheni grabbed the attendant closest to him by the lapels of their uniform.

"Why the hell aren't we moving?" he yelled.

"How in the galaxy should I know?" the attendant blathered in wide-eyed panic. "That's the captain's decision. I just serve the canapés!"

Sheni let the man go and hurried down the steps after the Garnidian. Maybe they'd know what was going on, why they weren't sailing back to the resort as fast as their hydrofoils could carry them. He found them hurrying back from the yacht's modest wheelhouse.

"Please tell me we're about to reverse out of here," Sheni gasped, already out of breath. He shouldn't have filled up on those crackers.

"So, this vessel doesn't actually go backward," the Garnidian explained apologetically. "And the engines need time to warm up after being put in standby for more than a few minutes. The captain's bringing them back online as quickly as she can."

A rusty metal hook at the end of an iron chain shot up from the water and hooked itself around the balcony railing.

"Not quickly enough, clearly!"

"Do you have any guns on board?" Gecki asked, stomping down the semi-exposed corridor behind him.

"Guns? *Guns?*" The attendant grew increasingly flustered. "Why would we have guns? *We're* not shooting any squid, are we?"

"Not for the molluscs, you imbecile – for the poachers about to raid your ship!"

She grabbed the hook tethering the smaller skiff to the yacht and, gritting her sharp teeth together as she strained, wrenched it off the balcony railing and chucked it back down into the sea. But no sooner did she do this than a loud smash could be heard from the dining room behind them.

"They're already on board," she snarled. "Godsdammit. You, waiter. Head back upstairs and make sure everyone's safe. Sheni and I will handle this."

"Will we?" Sheni asked.

"Well, the alternative is we *don't* handle this. That sound any better to you?"

Sheni reluctantly followed Gecki down the balcony and peered through the first of the windows looking into the dining room. It was conjoined with the reception area he spotted earlier, divisible by a set of walls that were presently retracted along their runners, obscuring a matching pair of holographic Qualian portraits. Sheni ducked as he spotted a pair of poachers striding down the length of the dining table, knocking carefully laid crockery onto the floor and pocketing anything that looked valuable. Which, on the yacht, was pretty much everything not nailed down. Judging by the poachers' shabby leather spacer duds, they were a professional outfit... just not a very profitable one.

"Gods," Sheni sighed. "Is this how the people we used to steal from saw *us?*"

"Probably," Gecki rasped quietly. "Except we didn't hurt animals, and we never killed anyone we didn't need to. I wouldn't put it past this lot."

Sheni winced as another plate got smashed.

"What are we going to do?"

"I'm gonna sneak around and try to flank them," she replied, crawling past him beneath the window. "You're gonna stay here and distract them."

"Distract them? How?"

"Stick your head out, or something. Make yourself a target. Just, you know, try not to get hit if they start shooting at ya."

"Your concern for my wellbeing is touching, as always."

"Well, we've already paid for your room for the fortnight..."

She slinked off down the hall, activating her camouflage

ability before she even reached the loungers by the stern. Her mint green scales shimmered a creamy white colour as she pressed her belly against the floor. Sheni cursed under his breath. Why couldn't Gecki be the distraction for once? Hers was the species who could regrow lost limbs, after all.

He raised his head to take another look at the poachers. One of them was checking under the table as if hoping to catch somebody hiding. Surely they had to know that most people were upstairs watching the squid leap about. He reckoned they also knew that the guests were trapped up there with nowhere to go.

Did the poachers have guns? Not that he could see, but the harpoons on their ships hardly filled him with confidence. Sheni wished *he* had one. A gun, not a harpoon. Not that he was all that great a shot, and he certainly didn't enjoy firing weapons, but the next few minutes would be a lot easier if any lead-based discourse wasn't a completely one-way conversation.

The window exploded outward as the poachers spotted him. Sheni ducked just in time to avoid getting a face full of glass. Tiny diamond-shaped fragments rained down the back of his Hawaiian shirt. Yep, they definitely had guns. Brilliant.

He crawled down the hall the way Gecki had gone, wincing as shards of glass cut into the palms of his hands. It's fine, he told himself. The resort has top-of-the-line medical facilities. If he got back to shore in one piece, they'd patch him up free of charge.

Clenching his jaw, he popped his head up again a few windows down. What he saw distracted him almost long enough to have his head blown off. Ducking back down as the second window erupted outward, he could have sworn he saw Alan sitting upright in the fruit bowl in the centre of the dining table, that goofy grin spread across his face like he was sledging down a snowy hill on a dinner tray. Nah, he had to be mistaken. Probably just a weirdly shaped pineapple, or maybe a really big grape.

One of the poachers' rounds punched a hole through the window's rubbery frame, inches from Sheni's ear.

"Any time now, Gecki," he muttered to himself.

There came a loud, meaty squelch moments later. Sheni grimaced as he heard the unmistakable sound of somebody choking on their own blood. A couple more shots were fired in quick succession, followed by another gory splat. There were two thuds as the second poacher hit the floor.

"You can come out now, human," Gecki rasped.

Sheni hesitantly rose to his feet and tiptoed through the closest door. Cutlery and candelabra were scattered everywhere. One of the fake pillars was doused with claret. Gecki stood next to the body of one of the poachers. He was slumped against the table with a glazed look in his eyes, bleeding over the fancy doilies.

"Don't act like I was hiding when I was the only one *actually* in any danger." Sheni shook pieces of glass from his shirt, then jumped as he discovered the dead poacher on the other side of the table. "Stars above, Gecki. You've decapitated him!"

"I was going for his throat," Gecki replied with a dismissive shrug. "Not my fault his head came with it."

"Is that all of them?"

A fiery roar from back where the tethering hook had caught on the railing. Sheni and Gecki rushed outside. The rickety skiff had ignited its thruster and was preparing to depart. One last poacher was crouching on its roof as if she'd just jumped down from the yacht's lower deck. Her black spacer jacket was noticeably nicer than the cheap leather rags on her colleagues, and the bony ridges of her skull were pierced with dozens of gold and silver rings. She raised her head and scowled at them.

"She looks like a right charmer," Gecki snarled.

Alan waddled out of the dining room to stand beside them. Sheni performed a double take. Maybe he hadn't been seeing things before. By the time he returned his attention to the poachers' ship it was already thirty metres away, skipping and spluttering over the waves toward the other two skiffs. Hurrying down the balcony, they watched as the three ships reconvened and dragged the lifeless corpse of a flying squid down the coast, back the way they came.

Finally, the yacht's engines vibrated with an embarrassed hum.

"What was all that about?" Sheni gasped as their boat made a beeline for the resort.

"I don't care," Gecki rasped with a wave of her claws. "I'm just glad it no longer has anything to do with us."

CHAPTER
THREE

Following the incident on the yacht, everybody on board wanted to buy them a drink to say thank you. Which would have been a much grander gesture had all the booze in the resort not already been free.

Still. Sheni didn't mind feeling like a hero for once. And the glances his crew were getting from the rich toffs swanning around Nova Elysia were definitely of a more positive nature than before. Everyone wanted to talk about the brave ruffians who'd saved them from the nasty pirates.

"I thought I was done with that kind of excitement," Xotl said while they were all sitting together at a hotel bar. The starfish was deep into their third coconut spritz. "Thank goodness we took out those goons without incurring serious injury."

"What are you on about?" Gecki rasped. "You were upstairs with the rest of the guests."

"Yes, I was. Exactly where you told me to be. And more than a bit frightening it was, too."

A slurping sound came from Sheni's beer. He looked down. Alan had stuck his straw in it.

"As for you, Alan," he said, wrinkling his nose as he returned Alan's straw to its rightful beverage. "I'm starting to think we need to put a leash on you. This is a classy joint. You can't go climbing every pillar and mast you come across."

One of Alan's bulbous eyes slowly swivelled upward to stare at the crystal chandelier suspended above their heads.

"Don't even think about it," Sheni warned.

The robotic automata working behind the counter rolled down with a fresh set of drinks courtesy of the snooty Oortilian from the boat. The slender blue alien raised his glass goblet of whiskey in acknowledgement from across the velvety, brass-trimmed bar; Sheni returned the gesture with a toast of his own.

"They pay you here, right?" Sheni asked the bartender. His shiny chrome chassis was in much better condition than Copper John's, the synthetic attendant at the Corpse & Casket.

"Of course," the robot replied in monotone. "The automata liberation movement ensured that all automata are awarded the same employee rights as organic citizens."

"Sure, yeah. I remember when the Ministry passed it into law a few years back. But that doesn't mean all of you are *actually* free, you know?"

"Unfortunately, you are correct. Many of my kind are still seen as nothing but thinking machines. But the people of Queflia have always been sympathetic toward the automata. I've worked at the Nova Elysia for twenty-six cycles, and they've always treated me as an equal."

"Well." Sheni tipped his fresh drink toward the barkeep. "Glad to hear it."

"Godsdamn poachers," Gecki rasped, twirling a piece of fruit around her drink with her claw. "Just as I was getting into watching those squid, too. And you just know the squid ain't gonna come back to that spot tomorrow, not after one of them got killed."

"Oh, yeah, because that's the real tragedy here," Sheni replied with a roll of his eyes. "They'll cancel tomorrow's excursion. Boo freakin' hoo. Those creatures were beautiful, and those psychos killed one just for a trophy, or for some exotic meat or whatever. Makes me furious, you know? And think how those Plillup must feel, the ones who have a... what's it called... some kind of relationship with them..."

"Weird?" Gecki suggested.

"Symbiotic," Xotl said pointedly.

"Yeah, that's it." Sheni shook his head. "Even if they're not as close as that Garnidian made it sound, it still must be awful for them. It's bad enough having a pet die, right? And mark my words – tomorrow those poachers will be back combing the waters for more squid to slaughter."

"Yeah, probably." Gecki shrugged and downed the rest of her drink in one. "But there ain't a lot we can do about that. And I'm sure Mr. Zelewyn notified the authorities. They attacked his resort's yacht, after all. Those poachers would be dumb to go fishing in that bay again any time soon."

"Yeah, maybe you're right. I just wish we could do more, you know?"

"More than take out two of the poachers and save a bunch of millionaires from getting robbed and murdered? You're setting the bar too high, Sheni. We're ex-spacers, not a squad of intergalactic superheroes."

Gecki slipped off her stool and scratched at the flaky scales under her chin.

"Up you get, crew. I've booked us a booth at diCarsko's

tonight. I'm starving, and they say the pterosaur steak is to die for."

S heni picked at his steak, shifting the pieces around the platter with his chopstick-style stabbing implement. Sure, it was probably the tastiest meat he'd ever eaten in his life, but for some reason he didn't have much of an appetite.

"I'll eat it if you won't," Gecki snarled, beckoning the food over with a curl of her claw. "Quick, though, before it gets cold."

"Sure, whatever." Sheni slid his platter across the table. "Knock yourself out."

"Is everything all right, Sheni?" Xotl asked. "You haven't contracted a stomach bug or something, have you?"

"No, I'm fine," he sighed. "Just can't stop thinking of those flying squid, you know? Well, not them so much as the Plillup down there in that sea, I guess."

"Those fish people were fine before you came to stay at Nova Elysia," Gecki rasped as she speared one of Sheni's meat bits, "and they'll be fine long after we've taken off to the stars again. Like I always tell you, bad things happen. Fact of life. Ain't no stopping it. We just do what little we can and move on."

"Sure, but it ain't just that." Sheni sipped his beer, which he found a lot more palatable than his steak. "This whole resort... it's a bit, you know, artificial, isn't it?"

Gecki paused in thought with a chunk of meat dangling from her spear-like utensil, then resumed eating.

"Well, yeah, course it is. Fancy stuff is always fake, ain't that kinda the point? Real life is gritty and grim."

"Exactly! But real life is also, well, *real*. It doesn't vanish like cotton candy in a puddle the second you stop paying for it. It's ever changing and yet eternal. And it's... well, I dunno." He shrugged. "I think it's worth witnessing."

"Sure, and we witnessed plenty of it today, didn't we? Poachers slaughtering a precious species. Doesn't get much more real than that."

Everybody sipped and slurped their drinks in contemplative silence. A member of diCarsko's wait staff glided by to collect their platters. Then Sheni perked up with such vigour it was as if he'd been struck by a cane rather than a thought.

"I'm gonna pay the Plillup a visit," he said with a satisfied grin. "That's it. I'm gonna hire one of those submersibles over by the dock and take it down to their city, see some of the *real* Queflia."

"Like hell you are," Gecki snarled. "That's outside of the resort. Private territory. And it's stupid dangerous, too. Last time I checked, you couldn't breathe water."

"So? The Plillup are amphibious. I'm sure it'll be fine." Sheni sniffed haughtily as he went to stand. "And I don't need your permission to go anywhere, thank you very much."

"Yeah, well, you ain't piloting anything tonight." Gecki yanked him back down into his seat. "You're drunk. Sleep on it. See if you still fancy sinking to the bottom of the ocean once the booze wears off."

"That's rich coming from you. You hardly ever pilot the *Silver Hart* these days unless you *have* had a few drinks!"

"Yeah, but in space there's a lot fewer things to hit. Now, you ordering a dessert or not?"

Sheni grumbled to himself and perused the holographic menu beaming out from the middle of their booth.

"Well, I can't very well miss out on their Queflian Milk Sponge, can I?"

CHAPTER
FOUR

T he sun was much too bright the following morning. The ocean glinted like a bed of polished jewellery. And, like a bed of shiny gemstones, all Sheni wanted to do was dive straight into it.

Instead, he shuffled down the sands with all the sluggish determination of a starving zombie. His brain ached. His mouth was bone dry despite the litre of water he guzzled before leaving his hotel room. He could practically smell himself cooking in the heat. But he'd made up his mind the night before, and like hell was anybody going to talk him out of it. Not even himself.

Gecki didn't know what she was talking about. *Dangerous*. As if. A city of quiet fish people just a few miles off-shore, and she was acting like he planned to fly their ship into a rabid Raklett den. Well, he'd show her. He'd have a lovely time integrating himself with the locals – the *true* locals – and be all the more fulfilled for it.

Besides, it would be nice to have a moment to himself for once. A brief respite from all the bothering and bickering.

"Hey, human," shouted a raspy voice. "Slow down, will ya? We don't all wear boots, you know."

Sheni groaned. Behind him, stomping through a shimmering heat haze, came Gecki's hulking green figure. She hopped from bare foot to bare foot, her short tail swinging erratically, as she hurried to catch up. Even reptilians knew better than to linger on hot sand.

"I thought you'd still be asleep," Sheni moaned.

"Yeah, well, I would be," Gecki rasped as she drew level with him, "but *somebody* made an almighty racket when they woke up, didn't they? I could hear you leaving your room from two doors down the hall."

"And you followed me all the way down to the beach?"

"Course I did." She gestured to her bare torso. "Doesn't exactly take me long to get ready in the morning, does it? And a captain's gotta make sure her crewmates don't go off and do something stupid. Reflects badly on her, otherwise."

"I'm not being stupid." He stomped on ahead. "I'm basically just taking one of their subs over to the nearest town. It's why they have a boat rental shop in the first place."

"Course, course. It's definitely not there so people with more money than sense can go gawp at the reefs, or anything."

"Well, maybe I'll do that too," Sheni exclaimed, hands raised. "It'll sure be a lot realer than, well, whatever *that* is."

He pointed back up the beach. A pair of curved Qualians were in the process of setting up a massive gazebo under which the galaxy's most embarrassing cross-species dance competition promised to take place.

Gecki growled under her breath and followed Sheni toward the rental facility. A pair of jet skis bobbed in the water close to its ocean-facing slip ramps, unclaimed by even the resort's earliest of risers. The neon sign installed above its front door wasn't lit. The yacht, still sporting a few nasty scuff marks from its earlier ordeal, was securely tethered to the pier running alongside it with both ropes and chains. The excursion planned for today had been cancelled, as expected.

Sheni shook his head clear of its hangover and knocked on the door. The sign said it was closed but he could see someone busying about inside. The attendant – an old bug with an especially wrinkly face – unlocked the door and peered up at him through the crack.

"Excuse me?" he asked. "Can I help you?"

"Erm, yeah, I hope so. I'm here to hire one of your subs, if that's all right."

The old bug's face wrinkled further.

"Oh. Even after yesterday?"

"Yep." Sheni grinned enthusiastically. "*Especially* after yesterday."

"Huh. Very well. I suppose you'd better come in."

Sheni and Gecki followed the slouched attendant into the rental shop, a largely rickety and wooden establishment compared with the rest of the resort. It smelled of mothballs and salt. Oxygen tanks and fishing rods hung from the walls. A golden fish swam amongst sea ferns in a large aquarium installed behind the counter. Through the speckled windows of the right-hand wall Sheni could see into the launching bay, an enormous, semi-exposed workshop in which more alien variations of jet skis, canoes, speedboats and private submersibles were stored and repaired.

"Stop this, Sheni." Gecki grabbed him by the arm. "Let's head back to the resort and grab a pair of loungers by the vertical pool, yeah? Or treat ourselves to an ice massage. Stars above, I'll even listen to that godsawful Oortilian band if you really insist."

"Man, you really don't want me to head out there, do you?"

"No, I don't. Those subs aren't safe, not even somewhere fancy like this. Not that this shop is quite as upmarket as the rest of Nova Elysia, mind you…"

"This rental place been here long?" Sheni asked the attendant, eyeing the warped wooden beams crossing overhead. "It *is* part of the resort, yeah?"

"Absolutely," the attendant replied with a proud, elderly smile. "We operated as a family-run business for years before the resort got built. The parent company offered my father a lot of credits for the land, and he negotiated a deal that ensured the continuation of this here shop as an on-site subsidiary. Mr. Zelewyn says it brings a sense of authenticity to Nova Elysia. So, was it a submersible you said you wanted, son? One seater, or two?"

"Just the one," Sheni replied, giving Gecki the side-eye.

"Make it two," Gecki growled. "This moron'll get himself killed without me there to steer the thing."

"Well, the sub's going on your room number." The attendant stepped out from behind the counter and pushed the wall with all the windows back on its rollers. "You break it, you bought it. Come pick out the one you want."

"What are you doing?" Sheni hissed at Gecki.

"Keeping you from making a stupid mistake," Gecki rasped back.

The attendant guided them through a semi-dismantled boat toward the rear of his workshop. Salty air and the sound of waves gently lapping against wooden supports crept up the slip ramps. At the top of the furthermost ramp was a long, torpedo-shaped cylinder the colour of storm clouds. Its transparent canopy hung open to one side. A pair of curved fins stuck out from its flanks and a single propeller jutted out the back.

The old bug slapped a clawed hand against its hull.

"This is the best two-seater I've got right this moment. Maximum speed of twenty knots. Capable of withstanding depths of up to—goodness me, how'd you get in there?"

Alan popped up from the front seat of the sub, a strand of seaweed draped over his head. Sheni spotted a series of sloppy footprints leading up from the water.

"I could hazard a guess," he said. "You got anything that seats three?"

Everyone jumped as the front door of the shop burst open behind them. The old attendant clutched a spindly hand to his thorax. A purple starfish waddled in carrying three armfuls of filter-compatible canteens.

"I'm not too late am I?" Xotl dumped their drink canisters on the counter. "Oh, good. You're still here. Apologies, Gecki. The bartender took a rather long time getting my drinks ready. I don't think he quite expected anyone to be awake."

"Or to be drinking this early," Sheni mumbled. "You got enough coconut spritzes there, Xotl?"

"Hopefully. This was all I could carry."

Sheni and Gecki raised a fluffy and scaly eyebrow respectively.

"What?" Xotl replied, their arms wilting slightly. "I've spent my whole life unable to get drunk. I've got a lot of catching up to do."

"I hate to say it," Gecki rasped to Sheni, "but I think we've been a bad influence."

"Hold on a minute," Sheni replied. "If you told Xotl to meet us here, then does that mean... you always intended to come on this trip with me?"

"No, I always intended to dissuade you." Gecki shook her head. "I still think you're a freakin' idiot. But family don't let each other be idiots alone."

Sheni gave her a wink and a light punch on the shoulder, then turned back to the attendant, who was still catching his breath after Xotl's unexpected arrival.

"Better make it a four-seater," he said with an apologetic shrug.

"Biggest one we've got is three," the attendant muttered, rubbing his bristly jaw. "But I reckon this little fellow here can sit on someone's lap. Come on, now. Out."

Alan blinked and smiled blankly, then hopped down to the floor. The attendant shoved the canopy of the submersible back into position and then tugged on a heavy chain beside it. Sheni watched as the two-seater chugged up toward the ceiling while a second vehicle, this one wider and flatter, shaped sort of like a stingray, slowly rotated down from amongst the rafters.

"There you go," the old bug said, clapping his hands together once the larger sub had thudded onto the ramp. "She's not quite as fast, but she'll go deeper. Should be able to carry the lot of you, too."

"Perfect." Sheni grinned. "Do we need to... you know..."

"Pay? Oh, no. Not here, anyway. It all goes on the room. Your account was scanned the moment you walked in. Nothing you need to worry about, son. Up you pop."

"All right, then..."

Sheni climbed up onto the wide flank of the submersible. Almost the entire top half of the sub had folded back on itself, revealing two seats up front – only the right one had access to steering controls – and a third seat at the rear where the sub narrowed. He dropped into the pilot's seat and studied the controls. They looked simple enough. Easier to wrap his head around than Xotl's customised dashboard on the *Silver Hart*, at any rate.

Xotl rolled into the rear seat. Between their stash of beverages and Alan, both of which were dumped unceremoniously into the back by an impatient Gecki, they were pushing the sub close to its weight capacity. There was an audible groan when Gecki finally collapsed onto the seat beside Sheni and pulled the canopy back down over their heads.

The attendant tapped on the glass, gave them an enthusiastic nod, and then pulled a rusty metal lever beside them. The stocks holding the submersible in place retracted and their vessel rumbled down the ramp, hitting the sea with a hard splash that shoved everyone forward in their seats. They bobbed on the surface for a moment, a thin film of water spilling over the canopy, listening to a steady *glug glug* sound coming from the vents.

"Go on, then. Hurry up." Gecki jabbed a claw at the controls. "It was bad enough skipping breakfast. I ain't planning on missing lunch."

Sheni took a deep breath (and in the process wondered how much oxygen their vessel actually had in its tanks), grabbed the twin-grip steering controls, and told himself he could do this. This was a rental sub designed for tourists, not professional oceanographers. He'd planned to come on his own, and now he had his whole crew with him. This was totally safe. Nothing could go wrong.

"Thanks for coming, guys. It'll be fun!"

"I'd say we shouldn't hold our breath," Gecki rasped grumpily, "but given you're driving, maybe that isn't such a bad idea..."

CHAPTER
FIVE

First they skimmed inches above the submerged shore. Then they dived as the slope stopped abruptly and the true sea began, deep and dark. Shimmering reflections on the surface turned to sinking sun beams turned to glimmers off polished rocks.

Sheni hummed the melody to Bobby Darin's *Beyond the Sea* the whole way down.

"Do you even know where you're going?" Gecki snarled.

"I looked up this Porto Kumasa place last night after we all went back to our rooms," he replied, his attention on the ocean depths ahead of them. "I've got a pretty good idea where it is."

"Yeah, so that's a no, then."

"Well I for one," Xotl said from the back, "am having a wonderful time. It's a true privilege to see the world from such a fresh perspective. And not from the pilot's seat for once."

A long, aggravating slurp followed.

"I'm sure those drinks are helping," Gecki replied. "You didn't think to grab us any while you were at the bar?"

"I've only got so many arms, Gecki."

"I don't know why you'd want to be drunk right now, anyway," Sheni mumbled. "I mean, even putting aside getting seasick. We can't exactly crack a window, you know? Look how beautiful everything is."

Narrow rays of sunlight still sliced down like fishermen's spears, but much of the environment through which the submersible passed was illuminated solely by the vessel's powerful flood lights. Gargantuan clumps of ancient rock coated with moss and algae and sea ferns and long grasses. The skeleton of a shark-like beast, picked clean. Whole steppes formed of weird, brittle, orange mushroom caps. Spiny blue sponges. Small fish of every shape and colour, some swimming alone, others sailing in enormous shoals a thousand strong. Bubbles escaping from gas pockets. Sheni knew that to their right, further south down the shoreline, lay an expansive stretch of hot pink coral, but they were headed in the wrong direction to check it out.

Alan observed all of this with his hands and eyeballs pressed right up against the glass.

"Yeah, it's beautiful, all right." Gecki crossed her arms. "But it ain't nothing I couldn't have seen in the big aquarium back in the resort's welcome lobby."

"Except this is real life, Gecki, not an artificial simulacrum of it. The difference between a natural diamond and one forged in a lab, you know?"

"Ooo, simulacrum. Fancy word, Sheni. But don't forget, *human*, that a fake can be even more valuable than the original. You know, to the right buyer. It's all a matter of perspective."

Sheni scrunched his brow and thought about this.

"How would that—"

"Just shut up and concentrate on not hitting the reefs, will ya?"

Sheni shook his head and guided the submersible under a natural archway stippled with bioluminescent fungi. Jellyfish as big as Alan billowed past them in a great cloud on the other side, their plasticky bells and long, black, barbed tentacles rubbing across the canopy like the bristles of a car wash. He checked the NavMap on the dashboard. According to an article he found on the extranet, they had to be getting close.

"Look over there," Xotl said, pointing an arm between the two front seats. "That's certainly not a naturally occurring structure, is it?"

Sheni listed the vessel ever so slightly to the right, and its flood lights washed over the remains of an ancient, half-collapsed bridge. He slowed the submersible, all of a sudden feeling like one of the recovery teams investigating the wreckage of the Titanic. Like they'd discovered something not seen by surface dwellers for hundreds, maybe thousands of years. The broken yet elegant stonework was covered in bone-white algae and black-shelled clams.

"This ain't the Plillup city, is it?" Sheni asked, concerned.

"Nah, looks too old," Gecki rasped. "S'pose water can do that to architecture, though. Erode it quickly. But I'd say it's either a relic from when the Plillup first built the place eight hundred years ago, or it's the ruins of some Queflian settlement from even further back in time."

"The Qualians aren't amphibious though, are they?"

"Not even remotely," Xotl replied between sips of coconut juice. "But Qualian society has flourished on Queflia for almost twenty thousand years. Shorelines change. The ocean reclaims everything, sooner or later."

"Hmm." Sheni slowly backed the sub away from the

bridge. "Either way, seems like an ideal place for a bunch of displaced colonists to start fresh. They've gotta be near, right?"

"Don't see any signposts," Gecki snarled irritably. "But I guess that's not the sort of thing you put up when you don't want to be disturbed."

Sheni ignored her and sent the submersible on a downward path under what remained of the ancient bridge. Darkness beckoned from the depths beneath. Plillup weren't nocturnal, or blind, and they couldn't see in pitch-black environments the way sharks and deep sea eels can. More solar beams radiated through the water ahead; the surface had to be a good couple of hundred metres above them now. Which meant they had to be right on top of Porto Kumasa. So where was it?

A wall of seagrass blocked their path, each bladed leaf two dozen metres tall, gently swaying as one against the underwater current. Sheni pushed through the aquatic meadow with the round nose of their submersible.

"Careful you don't get the motors tangled up in these weeds," Gecki rasped. "I ain't going outside to untie us."

"Stop worrying so much," Sheni replied. "Besides, if we get stuck we'll just tie a string around Alan and let him float up to the surface like a buoy. Someone would come along and rescue us eventually."

"Rescue a bunch of stranded spacers, really?"

"A bunch of *rich* stranded spacers."

"Yeah, good point. Down here in the darkness, it's easy to forget we ain't still up in the cosmos..."

"Erm, friends?" Xotl interjected. "Have I had one too many coconut spritzes, or is everybody else seeing an assortment of weird lights?"

Sheni switched off the submersible's flood lights and squinted through the grassy gloom.

"No, it's not just you..."

Half a dozen circles of white light permeated the meadow at odd angles to one another, and another twenty or thirty smaller lights floated eerily on the periphery.

"Turn us around," Gecki snapped. "Those are lures. You know, the kind predators use."

"Predators? You mean, like an anglerfish or something? I dunno, Gecki. It's just a bunch of lights. Doesn't have to mean something scary..."

"It ain't the light on an anglerfish you need to worry about," Gecki snarled, gripping the dashboard with her claws. "It's all the spiky stuff directly beneath it..."

Sheni, whose mind was suddenly filled with the image of needles sharp enough to puncture submarines, went to jerk the steering unit hard to the right. Xotl leaned forward and wrapped one of their arms around Sheni's own.

"Wait. Those lights don't belong to any fish."

"Are you sure?"

"Trust me. There are times when having a dozen eyes spread over five limbs can be useful..."

The last few leaves of seagrass peeled back from their canopy. Sheni readied himself for a colossal deep-ocean beastie to chomp down on their submersible. But his hands relaxed and fell from the controls. Xotl was right. Gecki was wrong. The lights weren't a lure at all.

"Porto Kumasa," he said, grinning. "Told you we'd find it, didn't I?"

Before them, a short drop off the cliff above which they presently floated, a sprawling town cascaded down levels of rocky steppes. The lights the crew had seen were either from bioluminescent lanterns installed along its curvaceous stone promenades or glowed warmly from inside the stained glass bubble-domes that dominated much of Porto Kumasa's districts. Hard stalks of coral stood as tall as the Eiffel Tower while gardens of their softer cousins flexed spongey polyps towards the sky. Sheni spotted few residents swimming from dome to dome, but his smile grew twice as wide as he watched more of the giant flying squid from yesterday glide through the water alongside manta rays, gigantic crustaceans and a hundred strange species of tropical fish.

"Admit it, Gecki," he said, nudging her. "This is a much cooler sight than anything back at the resort."

"I dunno, Sheni. A free buffet sounds pretty cool right about now." Gecki rolled her good eye as a pillar of bubbles gurgled up past their canopy. "But sure. Yeah. I guess it's pretty neat. So now we've seen it, how about we turn this thing around and get back to where the grub is?"

"Don't be ridiculous. We only just got here. I want to take a closer look."

"Be careful, Sheni," Xotl spluttered. "You heard what the excursion guide said. The people of Porto Kumasa are a rather reclusive sort."

"I'm not trying to catch one to bring home with us, Xotl! Stars above. I just want to see how the locals live."

"Oh, yes," Gecki rasped, "and that's never done anyone any harm…"

Keeping their velocity low, Sheni pushed the submersible over the edge of the cliff and down toward the subaquatic town. An almost spherical lobster-like creature, nesting amongst the kelp where the cliff began to level out again, scuttled out of their way; a pair of tubular worms the size of Sheni's socks took flight shortly after. Orange light flickered against the left side of their vehicle as they approached the first of the glass domes, and when Sheni glanced across he saw a splash of magma splutter up from inside a bubbling geothermal fissure. The whole settlement was probably powered on vents just like it.

"The architecture is fascinating," Xotl said, still facing the town. "So robust and yet so ornate. But I suppose one has to become pretty good at it when your species lives at the bottom of the sea."

"Bathypelagic fabrication," Alan giggled.

Sheni had to agree – with Xotl, that is. The designs of the Plillup houses were staggeringly beautiful in their ornate simplicity. Most were semi-circular and single storey, but the domes would overlap like soap bubbles conjoining, and spindly staircases of copper and coral could be seen linking one to the next through their round, starfish-adorned windows, which too were trimmed with cursive, gold-tinted nickel. It was all very *Art Nouveau*, a late nineteenth century style Sheni recalled from the retro posters and metro stations of Paris. He wondered if they forged all the glass and metal using the boiling geothermal vents or if they had to venture onto land to do it.

"Hold up a moment," Gecki rasped. "Someone's got their eye on us."

A pair of flying squid swam to a stop a couple of hundred metres away from them, above a dome topped with a tower of pearls. Each had a small rider straddling their mantle, though they were too far away for Sheni to get a good look at, and their long tentacles were shielded with copper sheaths and decorated with ribbons that drifted in the water like technicolour kelp.

"Better steer clear of that part of town, then." Sheni banked the submersible to the left. "Not to worry. There's a docking bay just down here, anyway."

A shimmering circle of light glittered on the curved exterior wall of a much wider rotunda shaped like an upturned pasta bowl. Three sled-like carts were tethered to the railing directly outside it. It was effectively like the forcefields in the docks on the Corpse & Casket space station, only this one kept the oxygen in and the water out. Most of it, anyway. More carts piled high with subaquatic foodstuffs could be seen parked within what Sheni guessed was a half-filled waterlock.

"I don't think that port is for us, Sheni."

"Oh, stop worrying. If they ask us to leave, we'll leave. What do you think they'll do, throw a trident at us?"

"Something like that..."

"I'm sure once they realise we're from the resort, they'll be just as interested in learning about us as we are about them," Xotl spluttered.

"Yeah, well, leave your drinks in the vehicle," Gecki snarled. "We don't know what counts for contraband round here."

Sheni eased the submersible toward the shimmering barrier, then killed the motors. Slowly it passed through the forcefield, nose first, and the transparent canopy was gradually split in half, one side bubbling as the barrier briefly superheated the water and the other clearing in trickling tributaries as it broke into air.

Their vessel tipped forward before plopping down into the relatively shallow lock on the other side, where it bobbed idly. Sheni let out a long breath, grinned triumphantly to his crewmates, and then released the canopy. It snapped back on its hinges like an overladen Bucking Bronco toy.

"Okay, gang." Sheni hopped out first, then clapped excitedly as he waded through the waist-high saltwater to the copper-trimmed steps on the other side of the waterlock. "This is what a *real* vacation looks like. Adventure, new experiences... actual *people*, not just brown-nosed hotel concierges! Hey there!"

Up top stood a small, scrawny, five-foot fish person. They had big black eyes blinking out of a wide, engorged head flanked by a pair of fins, glittery teal scales that covered every inch of their scarcely-clothed torso, and a basket of plump sea cucumbers clasped in their webbed hands. Sheni waved up at them as he climbed the steps. The Plillup dropped their cargo and sprinted out of sight.

"We shouldn't be here," Gecki snarled. "Let's get back in the sub and leave."

"Nonsense," Sheni replied. "We just caught the poor guy by surprise, that's all. They're probably not used to visitors."

Gecki, Alan and Xotl joined Sheni at the top of the steps and together they strolled past the carts the frightened Plillup had been in the process of unloading. Most contained stacks of vegetation – kelp, algae, bulrushes and horsetails – but there were a few small crustaceans and fish amongst the haul, too. Everything smelled very, well, *fishy*. Sharp light bounced off the pool and danced in eccentric patterns over the matte concave walls leading to the circular doorway at the far end of the chamber.

Sheni went to pull the tarnished metal lever beside the door, then hesitated. Gecki was tilting her head at him in a way that got his back up.

"Let's hope it's not a million gallon tank of water on the other side," she rasped. "I'm telling ya, this world ain't made for us. Nova Elysia, on the other hand – that very much *is*. And right now we're paying for a bunch of stuff we ain't getting, you hear me?"

"It's an all-inclusive resort, Gecki. Just order twice as much of everything when we get back."

He yanked the lever down and the spherical door split apart like two fans of metal leaves. Everyone's eyes grew wide, except Xotl, whose suckers puckered. As many as two hundred Plillup in varying shades of turquoise and teal went about their daily lives in this colossal bauble alone. Balconies of pink-orange coral and barnacled stone were decked out with railings of looping, calligraphic bronze. Pearls liberated from clams the size of a house had been stacked together to form an abstract statue in the centre of the chamber around which traders sold the goods imported via the waterlock. Plillup-related news bulletins were delivered from holo-drones hovering around the upper floors. A low, sorrowful moaning sound, sort of like whale song, filled the air, though nobody local appeared to react to it. Every visible surface was decorated with swirling, elfin flourishes. Sun beams refracted through the stain glass ceiling in the largest and most beautiful multicolour prism Sheni had ever seen.

"This is incredible," Xotl spluttered, bending backward, their five limbs rigid with awe.

"See, guys?" Sheni spun around with his arms out wide as if he could grab everything, pull it closer. "I told you this would be worth—"

Six Plillup guards dressed in skin-tight shark-leather armour hurried to intercept them. Each rode on the back of a scuttling purple crustacean the size of a rhinoceros with serrated front pincers powerful enough to crush an Alpha Rhoden in half. They rapidly surrounded the surprised crew of the *Silver Hart* and pointed their pikes at everyone's throats, beak, or gormlessly smiling face.

"—it."

Sheni gulped hard and raised his hands in surrender. Alan and Xotl followed suit.

"Bravo, Sheni. Great job." Gecki bared her teeth and clapped sarcastically. "We've had some frosty receptions in our time, but we've never been arrested quite *this* quickly before."

CHAPTER
SIX

The Plillup of Porto Kumasa shrank back from the outsiders being escorted through the town, peering out curiously from holes in the coral pillars and ushering their children back through kelp-curtained doorways. Sheni tried smiling at a couple of them, but their only response was to retreat further.

This wasn't exactly how he'd envisioned their visit going. But maybe if he could talk to someone, he could convince them he was only here to help, that this was all one big misunderstanding. Unfortunately, when he tried explaining this to the guards riding the giant lobsters, one of them jabbed him in the arm with their pike hard enough to draw a tiny bead of blood.

Gecki snarled and growled to herself as she stomped along beside him. Xotl rotated from arm to arm without a word, though Sheni could tell the starfish was terrified from the rapid way their suckers dilated and contracted. At least Alan didn't seem too concerned by their present predica-ment. His eyes continually rotated like a pair of Lazy Susans to look at every statue and fish they passed.

Despite his own mounting anxieties, Sheni remained transfixed by his subaquatic surroundings. How could he not be amazed by a city under the sea? Past the bustling and beautiful town square, they were escorted down a wider glass tunnel bridging it with the next dome along. Some of the tunnel segments were plastered, with coils of green and brown vines painted on them. Clumps of seaweed dangled from where the joints had leaked. The lights of other domes erected on the neighbouring coral shelves twinkled in distorted hexagons. Sheni supposed he should be grateful the locals had considered his species and hadn't dragged him back out the waterlock to drown.

A large two-finned shark swam alongside their group on the other side of the glass tunnel, watching them with a beady black eye. Sheni wondered if it was in league with the Plillup, or if it was a Pavlovian response, having been trained to expect dinner whenever it saw someone come this way.

He turned to Gecki and whispered, "The Plillup can't speak to fish, right?"

She fixed him with a glare cold enough to freeze a forge.

"You're a mammal. Does that automatically mean you can talk to pigs?"

"Yeah, all right. Screw me for asking, right?"

"No, screw you for ruining our vacation!"

"Quiet," one of the Plillup guards snapped, brandishing his pike at Sheni's neck.

At the end of the tunnel was another door that fanned aside upon their approach. More guards with pikes. Some with short swords and self-repeating crossbows, too. No 'modern' weaponry Sheni could see, though. This didn't surprise him, and it hardly reflected on the Plillup town's level of technological prowess. The colony had arrived on

Queflia in a spaceship, after all, and that had been eight hundred years ago. Pirates might not take such precautions in their skiffs and space stations, swinging their loaded rifles around like they were no more dangerous than baguettes, but any sensible society knew better than to permit guns in a community where a single stray bullet might bring the weight of an ocean down on their heads.

Sheni got the immediate impression this was some kind of political headquarters. Plillup administrators in wetsuit-like uniforms patted webbed hands over waterproof computer terminals with heat-sensitive touch screens. Senior warriors stood arguing around holographic maps, presumably of the seabed surrounding the town. But the main focus was unquestionably the throne sitting atop a stepped platform positioned at the rear of the chamber, a whirlpool of gold whiplash curls and delicate flourishes with a panoramic view of a black oceanic trench for a backdrop.

The crew of the *Silver Hart* were forced to kneel – or in Xotl's case, flop – in front of the throne. Its occupant was a Plillup like everyone else in Porto Kumasa, but twice as large in every parameter and dressed in a fine, flowing robe of red cotton with a lining of yellow citrine gemstones. Sheni wondered whether the Plillup elected the largest members of the tribe to be their leaders, or if their species had a hierarchical caste system, like ants and bees. The super-size kingpin finished his conversation with the diminutive courtier jotting down notes beside him and turned to face his audience.

"What is this?" he asked in a shrill, warbling voice.

"We caught these poachers sneaking into the Market Quarter, Lord Bol'glossa," said one of the guards riding a mega-lobster. "A gatherer witnessed them break in via the Elkhorn portal. Fortunately we could apprehend them before they did any real damage."

"Woah, hold on a second." Sheni knelt up straight and raised his hands in dissent. "We're not poachers. And we didn't break into anything. The portal thingy was open when we got there!"

"Silence," another guard said, jabbing him in the back with the tip of his pike. "How dare you speak before Lord Bol'glossa without invitation!"

"This ain't gonna be a trial, Sheni," Gecki rasped to him out the corner of her mouth. "We've skipped straight to the godsdamn sentencing."

"Poachers in Porto Kumasa." Lord Bol'glossa shook his bloated head from side to side; his jowls and fleshy whiskers flowed back and forth slowly as if he were submerged in water. "As if it wasn't bad enough that you spoil our waters and slaughter our kin. You violate our home as well."

The leader of the Plillup leaned forward in his chair and squinted at their group. Sheni wondered if their species' eyes were better suited for seeing underwater. Or maybe Lord Bol'glossa was just particularly short-sighted.

"What are you? A Kerulian without feathers, or a Luethian with a deficiency of arms?"

"I'm a human," Sheni replied. "From Earth. Or New Terra now, I guess."

"Haven't heard of you. And what about this scaly creature – what are *you* supposed to be?"

Gecki bared her teeth and snorted through her nostrils.

"I dare say there are more scales on your fat behind, *Lord*, than there are on all of me."

"But mine are the right *kind* of scales," Lord Bol'glossa

replied with a disdainful sneer. "You reptilians are all the same. Combing the galaxy in search of worlds to conquer. Think you own whatever you set your horrid yellow eyes on, don't you?"

His scrutiny continued down the line of detainees, only to be cut short as he performed a double-take.

"Release that one," he suddenly shouted, pointing a finger at Xotl. "Don't you fools recognise an Estroidean? Their kind certainly aren't in league with the poachers, are they? And for the love of *Poruto*, let their pet go free, too."

The guards hurried to pick Xotl and Alan up off the floor. Xotl was technically a Xocha, not an Estroidean, but it was an easy mistake for a non-starfish shaped species to make. Estroideans were the Xocha's aquatic cousins, genetically speaking, and Lord Bol'glossa presumably thought that meant they weren't likely to go around harpooning other people's squid.

Unsurprisingly, Xotl wasn't quick to correct him.

"My friends have nothing to do with the poachers," they spluttered. "They came here hoping to help."

"I shall be the judge of that," Lord Bol'glossa replied. "Guards, take these two back to the Market Quarter. Ensure our guests are well-fed and cared for."

Xotl flapped an arm backward to look at Sheni and Gecki as they were escorted out of the chamber. Alan tottered along with a blissful smile stretched across his face. Sheni hoped the guests in question actually *were* Xotl and Alan, and not a bunch of crustacean dignitaries about to receive a free sushi lunch.

Everybody in the chamber was silent while they waited for Lord Bol'glossa to speak, even the administrators and security chiefs working on the other side of the dome. Sheni felt like he ought to say something, to plead his and Gecki's innocence, but knew he'd only receive a spear tip in the spine for his efforts.

"You land-dwellers think you can have whatever you want," Lord Bol'glossa said. "Do you even know how many squid you've killed this past half cycle? Fourteen. *And* two riders. Have you any idea how long it takes for a squid to reach adulthood? How many squid are born each annum? No, of course you do not. You simply take and take what isn't yours until there is nothing left. And then you move onto the next ocean or the next world and you do the same thing there. We have another word for a poacher here. *Parasite*."

"Lord Bol'glossa, please." Sheni expected a violent rebuttal in response to speaking up, but none came. "I swear to you, we have nothing to do with the poachers hunting in these waters. I'm as appalled by what the poachers are doing as you are. We actually saw them kill one of your squid just yesterday. That's why we came to Porto Kumasa. Not to take anything from you, but to see if there's anything we can do to help."

"That, and to wonder at your *beautiful* architecture," Gecki added.

"You're not helping," Sheni hissed.

"So you know about the death of Hefu, the youngest of that squad," Lord Bol'glossa replied angrily. "That proves you're in league with the poachers!"

"No it doesn't! We were on board a yacht at the time. You know, the one that sets out from the Nova Elysia resort on the shore? In fact, we had to fight to keep the poachers from taking over the boat, too."

"I killed a couple," Gecki rasped, graciously bowing her head. "You're welcome."

Lord Bol'glossa waggled his whiskers incredulously.

"Look at the two of you. You're covered in scars and your

clothes are scuffed and you speak like common peasants. You seriously expect me to believe you're patrons of that horrible resort?"

"Yeah, coz we are. It's the future, man. Not everybody who's rich has to be wearing a suit and tie, you know?"

"Yes, well." Lord Bol'glossa sank back into his throne and sneered at them. "I can imagine poaching *is* very lucrative."

"Your lordship, please." Sheni gave a tired shrug. "How are we supposed to prove to you we *aren't* poachers? We just want to help. Let us. How about we reach out to the Ministry for you, get them to put a stop to the hunting?"

"The arrogance to think we need your help. That we'd even *want* it! You don't think we know how to contact this precious Ministerium of yours?" He waved a hand at the waterproof terminals. "Of course we do. We trade. We import translator chips, even. We simply have no interest in inviting outsiders to meddle in our affairs."

"But maybe if more people knew what was happening here, they would—"

"Still your tongue," Lord Bol'glossa snapped. "*We* know what is best for the Plillup of Porto Kumasa – not this Ministerium of So-Called Cultured Planets, and certainly not a pair of opportunistic scoundrels like you."

Sheni glanced at Gecki, who shrugged.

"There ain't no convincing some people," she rasped.

"Coming to Porto Kumasa was clearly a mistake," Sheni said, nodding in defeat. "You don't want us here. We get it, you know? That's cool. Just let us be on our way."

"Oh, we won't keep you here. We have no interest in wasting precious resources on imprisoning outsiders."

"Thank the stars," Sheni sighed. "For a moment I thought you were—"

Lord Bol'glossa clicked his webbed fingers together and the guards rushed forth to grab Sheni's arms. A blade was quickly thrust under Gecki's throat to keep her from slaughtering their assailants. Lord Bol'glossa leaned forward from his throne and squinted at them down his jowls.

"Feed them to Mother Maw."

CHAPTER
SEVEN

S heni tried to tear open the kelp bars of their cage, but the pneumatocystic blades were as firm as two-inch-thick leather. Even Gecki's claws weren't sharp enough to cut through.

"I reckon there's metal underneath," she muttered as she gave up.

Following Lord Bol'glossa's judgement, Sheni and Gecki had been ushered down more finely decorated, nickel-trimmed tunnels to a much smaller dome filled with strange bladder sacs and copper manacles. The curved walls were all metal, no glass. There they'd been given organic-looking masks and ordered to strap them over their heads. Sheni had resisted at first, believing them to be some kind of torture device. Then he realised what they actually were – rebreathers, ones which allowed them to see, hear and speak underwater. The Plillup were taking them outside.

Not before the guards had jabbed and prodded them inside the cage of kelp suspended from the dome's ceiling, though. Once incarcerated, water sloshed up from pumps installed in the floor. Only then did the metal segments of the dome peel back on themselves piece by piece, folding away like the fanned leaves of the town's lever-operated doors.

The cage had been effortlessly pushed outside by a pair of Plillup guards, then brought to a floating stop a short distance from Porto Kumasa's township. Sheni counted another dozen armed Plillup standing watch nearby. Before them stretched a black fissure in the seabed, a couple of hundred metres wide and unfathomably deep. Thousands of Plillup locals patiently gathered on neighbouring coral caps and steps chiseled into the precipice of the great chasm. It struck Sheni that the whole population had come to see them perish.

Well, why not? Bring the kids, buy some popcorn – you know, make a day of it.

Sheni gave the kelp another desperate tug and then clung to the bars with his eyes closed. Without something to grab onto, he found his legs floating up above his head.

"I could have done with a bit of help back there, you know, instead of you just winding everyone up."

"Nah, what would be the point? Lord Whats-His-Name had made up his mind before we even reached his throne. People like him don't know their butt from their barnacles."

"Yeah, well, maybe if you'd *tried*, we could have convinced him to let us leave. Via the waterlock, I mean."

"Look at him, Sheni. Pompous blob probably hasn't left his chair in weeks. Does he seem like the listen-to-reason type to you?"

Sheni looked out the back of their cage. Lord Bol'-glossa sat on his throne by the window of his dome only a couple of dozen metres behind them. Best seat in the house. He had a big smile on his smug face as two attendants dabbed him down with saltwater. The way it dripped off his fleshy whiskers made him look as if he were sweating profusely.

"No, I guess not." Sheni sighed and leaned against the kelp. "I'm sorry, Gecki. It was a stupid idea to pilot the sub down here. This is all my fault. Again."

"I told you, didn't I? Local culture ain't all it's cracked up to be. People who build houses underwater *want* to be left alone."

"You seem oddly calm." He furrowed his brow. "Normally you'd tear off my head for dropping the ball like this. You've thought of a clever way out of this, haven't you?"

"Nah. We're stuck in here. But the way I see it, the Plillup aren't that big, right? So maybe this Mother Maw they mentioned ain't as terrifying as they make out."

The guard floating to the left of their cage chuckled.

"Hey, what's so funny?" Gecki rasped.

"You topsiders are all the same," the guard replied. "You think you're better than us, more knowledgable, more capable. But you don't know the first thing about our world, do you? You think everything works the same down here as it does up top, only wetter."

Sheni peered through the bars of kelp at the flying squid circling the waters directly above the chasm. Each had a Plillup rider on its back. They were huge, probably as big as the giant and colossal squid species had been back on Earth. Abyssal gigantism, that's what the scientists called it.

"Your squid friends," he asked. "They're connected to this Mother Maw creature somehow, aren't they?"

The guard chuckled again.

"You could say that." His black eyes scrutinised the prisoners. "I wonder how this will translate, but I must ask: are you familiar with extreme sexual dimorphism?"

"Well, that's a pretty personal question..." Sheni blinked

as he realised what the Plillup meant. "Oh, I think I know what you're on about. There was a species of anglerfish back on Earth, and the females were something like fifty times as big as the males. The boys were basically just, like, swimming gonads."

"Fifty times." The guard mulled this over. "Yes, that sounds about right."

Sheni and Gecki shared a glance, then peered down into the cavernous pit beneath their feet.

"Forget what I said," Gecki rasped. "On second thought, I reckon Mother Maw's *way* worse than her name suggests."

They both jumped as a series of weighty bass notes blasted out from copper pipes installed amongst the coral on the other side of the chasm. Sheni didn't know if the notes meant something to the people of Porto Kumasa, like this was the opening melody of their national anthem or whatever, or if it was the equivalent of a dinner bell. Either way, most of the Plillup in attendance began to applaud.

Bubbles escaped from the bladder sacs tied to the cage and their prison began its slow descent into the pit. Sheni went back to tugging on the bars.

"Do you think Xotl and Alan are watching?" he asked.

"Oh, I imagine so. Probably being treated to a fine meal of oysters and champagne, too."

"Better than all four of us dying, I guess."

"If you say so. Gods, the thought of Alan taking over as captain of the *Silver Hart* makes my scales shiver..."

"Will you stop being so calm and *do* something?"

"Do what? I ain't chewing through that freakishly thick seaweed. And even if we did break out, where do you think we're gonna go?"

The damn lizard had a point. They couldn't swim down, obviously. Up was optimistic given the numerous squid riders circling Mother Maw's pit. And even sideways wasn't much of an option. No way could the two of them over-power a thousand angry fish-people.

Inside the cage or out, they were stuck down here. Breaking free would simply reclassify them from an appe-tiser to a pair of fun-size snack bites in the eyes of Mummy Squid.

"What do you think's better?" Sheni gulped. "To see this giant squid beast of theirs before she eats us, or to scrunch our eyes shut and not see it coming?"

"Not see it, probably."

"Oh well. Too late."

A pair of long, fleshy, squid-like feelers reached up from the darkness below. Each had to be at least sixty metres in length and was lined with hundreds of chitin-ringed suck-ers. And the further she stretched toward the sunlight dancing across the waves, the more of the creature known as Mother Maw came into view. Orange eyes with rectangular pupils the length of telephone poles. A hooked, reddy-brown beak equal in size to a Plillup's dome. A purple and pink tentacle as wide as the *Silver Hart* that snaked out from a completely separate crack in the rock. And those were only the parts of her Sheni could make out in the inky gloom. Abyssal gigantism was putting it mildly. The lady kraken was so gargantuan, he doubted she could even leave the network of subaquatic caverns she called a home.

Sheni was glad he was totally submerged in seawater. Nobody would ever know he'd wet himself.

"Now I've thought about it," Gecki said, furiously gnashing at the kelp. "Maybe losing a few teeth ain't the worst thing in the world."

"Holy mother of..." Sheni tugged at the bar next to her. "It's like if Xotl had a baby with Godzilla!"

Gecki scrunched up her snout in confusion as she slashed and chewed.

"Do I know him?" she asked.

The Plillup lining the pit continued to clap and cheer as the cage sank deeper and deeper. Sheni could no longer see Lord Bol'glossa watching from his chamber window. In fact, soon they wouldn't be able to see any of their audience, save for the guards riding the squid directly above. Between the bars of their cage and the lip of the fissure, their view was becoming increasingly leviathan in nature.

Sheni tugged and wrung the kelp, but he may as well have been trying to rip a rubber tyre with his bare hands.

"Hurry up, Gecki!"

"I'm hacking as hard as I can, human! Why has your species evolved to be so freakin' feeble, huh?"

One of the kraken's clubbed feelers brushed the side of the cage. Sheni yelped and kicked backward through the water. It was prodding them downward, in the direction of her beak. He grabbed hold of two bars on the opposite side and tried to wriggle past them.

"What are you doing?" Gecki hissed.

"Seeing if I can squeeze through!"

"Well, don't! A captain never abandons her crew. And neither should her crew abandon their captain!"

"Then we'll both die!"

"That's just a risk we'll have to take."

Another series of bass notes – shorter and faster this time – trumpeted out from the copper organ pipes before Sheni had a chance to reply. The Plillup around the pit immediately lost interest in the execution, propelling themselves from the stone steps and coral caps and gliding to the safety of their residential domes. Even the guards riding the flying squid abandoned their positions and rocketed toward the surface.

"What's happening?" Sheni asked.

"Poachers," Gecki rasped. "You know, the *real* ones. I reckon they've struck again."

The feeler trying to wrap itself around their cage retracted into the abyss. Sheni peered down just in time to spot the kraken's eye rush past the mouth of the cavern at the bottom of the fissure.

"Looks like Mrs. Maw has lost her appetite, too."

"Maybe she's been trained to associate those noises with danger," Gecki said, tearing into the kelp. "She must be incredibly valuable to the Plillup here. I imagine they only have the one."

"Gods, you'd hope so, wouldn't you? I wonder how they—"

"Stop thinking and get us out of here, you idiot!"

They ripped and tore, but no matter how ravaged and threadbare they made it, the seaweed simply wouldn't break apart... and the cage still sank toward where the kraken's beak had lurked moments earlier. Something told Sheni that Mother Maw wouldn't be half as reluctant to chow down on them once they'd crossed the threshold of her cavern.

"Stars above." Sheni pointed through the churning waters. "One of the squid riders is coming this way. I reckon they're gonna finish us off themselves. Skewer us through the cage, or something."

Gecki squinted through the waterproof mesh of her mask and grinned.

"Nah. If that's a squid, it's gotta be the weirdest one *I've* ever seen..."

Chopping through the water in haphazard zigzags came

Sheni's hired submersible. Sheni laughed in manic disbelief. Xotl and Alan peered out from the transparent canopy as the sub descended into the pit after them.

"So much for champagne and oysters, huh?"

The sub came to a clumsy stop beside the cage. Xotl's arms flapped about as they struggled with the uncomfortable controls.

"...daft machine," they said, their spluttering voice suddenly cutting through the water from the sub's speakers, "too many buttons and not enough handles... Oh, hello. Comms are working again, thank goodness. I assume you would like some assistance?"

"If you'd be so kind," Gecki snarled. "I don't suppose Sheni splurged for the deep sea salvage package when he hired that sub, did he?"

"Screw me for thinking we'd be sightseeing, not recovering the Titanic," Sheni sighed.

More bubbles escaped from the bladder sacs attached to the cage, which sank lower into the kraken's pit.

"There is another slight issue," Xotl continued. "I can't open the canopy of the submersible to let you in. It goes without saying that Alan and I would drown."

Alan's face was pressed to the roof of the sub, his eyes swivelling to study the bioluminescent coral and his smile as wide as the Panama Canal.

"We'll solve that problem later," Gecki rasped. "Right now we need to figure out a way to break this cage open. Teeth and claws ain't gonna cut it. Literally. Either that, or you've gotta give this whole cage a tow."

"We do not have a tow cable," Xotl replied matter-of-factly.

"Probably wouldn't work anyway," Sheni replied. "Even

if we could tether ourselves somehow, the line would just get cut by the submersible's motors..."

Sheni and Gecki shot each other a sharp look.

"Xotl, back up to the cage," Gecki ordered. "Slowly. Don't carve us up along with the kelp, you know?"

"Are you sure about this?" Xotl replied. "If the propeller fans get clogged up, we'll all die down here."

"That's a risk we'll have to take," Gecki reiterated. "Just do it."

Xotl turned the submersible around so that it faced away from the cage, then slowly backed up to the kelp bars Gecki had already weakened. She and Sheni retreated as far back as the cage allowed. The sub's two motors were positioned close together at the rear of the vessel, and though they were largely encased in protective plastic Sheni could see the propellers sucking in water. They weren't spinning as quickly as they would if the sub were going forward, but he crossed his fingers and hoped it would be enough.

"Closer..." Gecki curled a claw toward her. "Closer..."

The rear of the submersible bumped into the bars of the cage. The kelp sagged inward slightly but didn't break. And the plastic casing around the motors kept them from getting clogged. Sheni's heart sank even faster than the cage. He supposed that's exactly what the casing had been designed for.

Xotl revved the motors, readjusted the sub's angle, reversed again. This time one of the propellers was lined up perfectly with the ragged bar of kelp. But still it couldn't reach.

And then one of the loose, trailing strands got sucked in.

It was only the width of a pinhead, but it snagged. The motor made a horrendous grinding sound as it fought to turn. The sub began to list to the right, rolling the whole cage with it. Sheni grabbed hold of whatever he could and waited for something important to explode.

The kelp tore in half with a short, sharp snap. The propeller devoured what remained of the seaweed and went back to spinning, albeit with a lot more grunting noises than before.

"Aha!" Sheni shouted. "You did it!"

"That's enough," Gecki rasped excitedly. "Get clear of the cage. We should be able to swim through now."

The submersible continued to reverse.

"Now go forward. Forward, you floppy-armed fool!"

"I'm trying," Xotl spluttered. "I can't make it switch gears!"

The motors kept coming toward them. Sheni glanced up and just about caught a glimpse of Alan clambering up toward the pilot seat. The submersible drifted to a stop inches away from their stomachs, then changed course, engulfing them in bubbles.

"That was a close one," Sheni sighed. He looked down and began to panic. "Speaking of close ones… we're almost at the bottom of the chasm!"

Gecki let out a snarl. They'd sunk further than they realised. One colossal orange eye peered up at them from the dark caverns below. They hurriedly swam out of the broken cage to where Xotl had brought the submersible to a weary stop.

"What should we do?" Sheni asked. "You heard what Xotl said. They can't let us in."

"I could pilot it back to the waterlock," Xotl suggested. "It was still open when we left. You could swim after us and then climb aboard in there."

Gecki pointed an agitated claw past Sheni's shoulder.

"I don't think we've got time for that…"

Sheni slowly floated around. One of Mother Maw's enormous club-shaped feelers had crept up behind him. Poachers on the prowl or not, someone was getting hungry.

"Quickly, hold onto something," Xotl spluttered.

Gecki dug her claws into the metal fin on her side of the submersible; Sheni stretched his torso across his own fin and held onto its edge as tightly as he could. Something told him a human grip wouldn't amount to much once they were jetting through the water.

"Go, Xotl," Gecki snarled. *"Go!"*

The sub picked up speed, but slowly. It wasn't used to carrying that much drag, and one of its motors wasn't operating at full capacity. The feeler drew closer, coiled tighter as if moving to grab them. Sheni dared to glance over his shoulder and watched their cage of kelp get crushed like a nut between the two mountainous mandibles of the kraken's beak.

"Floor it, Xotl!" he screamed.

The feeler, mere metres from the canopy, cast a bleak shadow as it constricted further. The submersible coughed and whirred out of the way seconds before the tentacle could crack it in half and haul the remaining pieces down into the abyss.

By the time Mother Maw relaxed her grip in disappointment, the crew were already out of the pit and racing as fast from Porto Kumasa as propellers could carry them.

CHAPTER
EIGHT

The submersible lurched onto the beach like a killer whale hunting a seal, its bent propeller emitting a high-pitched whine and its motors coughing like it had the flu. Sheni rolled onto the sand, tore off his semi-organic mask and gasped for air. On the other side of the sub, Gecki dropped into the lapping surf and left a seven foot crater in the shoreline.

The canopy snapped open on its hinges a second later. Alan hopped out, smiling like a kid who's just got off a roller coaster and is already desperate to queue up and ride it again, and scampered up the shore toward the trees. Xotl was slightly less enthusiastic following the crash. They extended one arm out of the submersible, clacked their beak in discomfort, and then proceeded to hobble dizzily from one arm to another across the nose of the vessel.

Sheni raised his head. The rest of his body refused to function. Hanging onto the sub for dear life as it sped through the waters had drained all the feeling out of him.

"Well, we ain't kraken food," Gecki rasped. "I guess we ought to be grateful for that."

"Now we're just lunch for the gulls," Sheni replied, staring up at the pterosaurs circling overhead.

"Oh stars," Xotl spluttered from on top of the sub. "All of my coconut spritzes. They broke in the crash."

Sheni couldn't help but laugh.

"How tragic, Xotl. They're just fizzy coconut water, you know? Hardly a bottle of Château Lafite 1869. Just cartwheel up to the resort and grab some more."

"Erm, yeah. About that." Sand rained off Gecki's head as she lifted it to study the beach. "Where is the resort, exactly?"

"Don't ask me," Xotl replied. "After that monster almost got us and the motors started to cut out, I just pointed the sub at the closest bit of land."

Sheni summoned the strength to stand up. Half of his person was caked with wet sand, and the other half was soaked through. He could have sworn one of the propellers had nicked his shin at some point during their tempestuous subaquatic voyage, and half expected to discover he was standing on just the one leg. But now, looking down, Sheni realised it was just a crab who'd decided to hitch a ride. He swatted it off and winced as saltwater trickled into the tiny red dot it left behind.

"My enviro-suit," Xotl spluttered, suddenly remembering themself. They bent their arms this way and that. "I think it tore in the crash. I can't see any damage, though. Are there any rips? Alan, get down from there and tell me if I've got any rips!"

Alan was halfway up the trunk of a palm tree when Xotl began panicking. He dropped to the ground, hurried back down the sand, and studied every inch of Xotl with his revolving eyes.

"Imperforate regalia," he gurgled, patting Xotl on the beak.

"Thank goodness," Xotl replied, relaxing their arms. "I'll take that to mean I'm okay."

"For now," Gecki snarled. "Where in the godsforsaken galaxy are we?"

Sheni squinted both ways down the beach. Lots of sand in either direction, but not much in the way of fancy cabanas and five-star spa rooms. A dense forest of palm trees and five-foot ferns blocked their way inland. The clear ocean was tranquil and empty, save for a couple of small islands way off in the distance.

"We're probably just a little further down the coast," Sheni said, knocking as much sand off his wet clothes as he could. "Thanks for getting us out of there, Xotl. We would have been screwed if you and Alan hadn't come along when you did. As for getting back to the resort – we can't have gone too far, you know?"

"Well, we ain't going back the same way we got here." Gecki gave the side of their busted submersible an irritated kick. "*And* all the electrics are dead, so we can't call for help. We ain't getting our deposit back for this piece of crap, that's for sure."

"So we walk back," Sheni suggested, worrying how much the cost of a new three-seater submersible would eat into his share of the crew's fortune. "I reckon we can still make it back in time for dinner. Not that it isn't *always* dinnertime in Nova Elysia, mind you."

Xotl curled one arm toward the west, the other toward the east.

"The question is," they spluttered, "which way?"

Sheni felt twice as hot under everyone's gaze as he did under the baking sun. This was his mess to fix. But until they got their bearings, one direction was as good as the other.

"This way," he said, strolling toward the east. "It curves toward the south, which is, erm, where I reckon we ought to be headed, yeah?"

Gecki stepped in front of him and jabbed a claw into the centre of his chest.

"Slow down there, mammal," she snarled. "Your track record of making sound decisions stinks worse than a steaming pile of muloch dung. I hardly think you should be the one choosing where we go next, do you?"

"That's fine, I just reckoned we could—"

"I mean, what were you *thinking?*" Gecki hissed through rows of sharp teeth. "That Garnidian on the tour yesterday specifically said that if we spotted a Plillup from Porto Kumasa wandering about on the rocks, we should *ignore* them. So what does clever little Sheni Dupont do? He rents a sub and sinks it to their reclusive colony at the bottom of the sea so he can say hello. But that's not enough for Sheni. Oh, no. The dumb human has to pilot it straight into their godsdamn town and get everyone fed to a freakin' kraken, too!"

"Just the two of you, actually," Xotl quietly interjected.

"Come on, how's that my fault?" Sheni considered his own question. "Well, piloting the sub down there was, sure, and docking in their waterlock. That's my bad, yeah. But I couldn't have known the Plillup would confuse us with the poachers, could I?"

"Of *course* you could! Stars above, Sheni – they're a hermit community. They have scarcely any contact with the rest of Queflia, let alone the wider Ministerium. It should have been obvious they'd freak out at a bunch of strangers barging into their home while their squid are getting slaughtered. The dumb fish don't know any better."

"Well, that's hardly their fault. You can't blame them—"

"I ain't blaming them! I'm blaming *you!*"

"Friends, please." Xotl carefully cartwheeled between them. "Arguing certainly won't get us any closer to the resort, will it? I say we follow Sheni's suggestion and continue this disagreement over unlimited piña coladas."

"We ain't going that way," Gecki growled. "For one, I don't trust Sheni's judgement. And two, guessing is never the answer, not 'less you want to get even more lost than you already are."

She pointed up at a rocky tor rising above the palm trees behind the shore.

"High ground. First we find Nova Elysia, *then* we find the way to go."

CHAPTER
NINE

The trees provided some respite from the harsh midday sun, at least, and it didn't take long for the seawater to dry from his clothes, though Sheni still found himself drenched in sweat. If only the hardened sand was as quick to vacate his person. He felt like a walking statue.

The rocky tor Gecki had spotted wasn't that far from the beach. A few hundred metres or so. Half a kilometre at most. But carving a path through the thick bracken, gnarly roots and towers of tropical mushrooms made for slow progress.

"Oh, I don't like this," Xotl spluttered anxiously. "There could be anything hidden under all this foliage. Trap door spiders. Venomous serpents. Sticks with splinters. You know what'll happen if something punctures my enviro-suit..."

"We ain't carrying you," Gecki rasped, raising her eye to the heavens.

"Don't worry so much," Sheni said, patting one of Xotl's arms. "That suit's a top-of-the-line model. We really splashed out on it after we sold the sword. It's gonna take a lot more than a pointy pebble to get through that, believe me."

"If you say so..."

They trekked uphill, brushing away vines and creepers while trying not to roll an ankle on the craggy, uneven terrain. It was hard, tiring work. Something cawed from a branch high above. Elsewhere, a critter yapped and scurried through the foliage in the opposite direction to them.

Sheni suddenly got the impression that their group was one person short. Gecki stomped ahead, and Alan could be identified by the rustling in the undergrowth. Xotl had stopped half a dozen metres back and was staring up at the coconuts hanging from a palm tree with a yearning look in their tentacles.

"Do you think if one of you shakes it enough," they asked, "it'll become something akin to a spritz?"

"Good grief, Xotl. You're the first person I've met who's capable of developing an alcohol dependency without ever having touched the stuff."

"I'm simply thirsty, Sheni."

"Then drink some water. You know, something you ain't allergic to!"

"That would be splendid. Have you got any?"

Sheni exhaled deeply. No, he did not. None of them was carrying food or drink of any kind. And whilst he could stomach being hungry, even having skipped breakfast like an idiot, they wouldn't get very far in this climate without first getting some decent liquids inside of them.

"I thought as much," Xotl continued. "Alan, would you be so kind as to climb that tree and retrieve a coconut for me?"

Their small green companion, who could barely be seen above the top of the ferns, blinked twice and then waddled toward the tree trunk in question.

"Alan, don't listen to Xotl." Gecki shook her head. "Xotl, you need water. *Fresh* water. Drinking something you're allergic to will only make you thirstier. You'll shrivel up like a dehydrated sea sponge."

"Besides, we're probably just a mile or two from the resort." Sheni waved Xotl up the hill. "By the time we're properly parched, we'll have access to all the coconut spritzes and rum punches we can drink."

"I suppose so." Xotl slowly cartwheeled from arm to arm. "There's no point in shaking seeds about when the real thing might be just around the corner."

"That's the spirit," Sheni said. "Or wine, or beer…"

They reached the base of the tor a few minutes later. The trees and ferns grew sparse as rocks replaced soil. Xotl placed the tip of each arm upon the loose stones as carefully as possible. Alan, on the other hand, was already halfway up the outcrop, scaling its near-vertical face like an alpine mountain goat.

"You'd better have an easier route in mind," Sheni grumbled.

"This way," Gecki rasped with an exasperated curl of her claw.

She led Sheni and Xotl further up the sloping hill, around the side of the tor itself, where stubby grass and damp moss squelched underfoot. The rock, light grey in colour and speckled with white, jutted out from the earth at a forty degree angle. Everybody except Alan doubled back on themselves and scaled the gentle incline to its peak above the surrounding tree canopies. Alan stood waiting for them at the end, smiling patiently, facing the wrong direction.

"Right, that's the hard bit over and done with," Gecki snarled. She marched toward the edge, already swinging her snout left and right. "Now we've just gotta... oh, godsdammit."

"What? What's wrong?" Sheni inched beside her, trying to avoid looking over the drop. "Ah. Yeah, that's an issue."

"You think? We're marooned on a freakin' deserted island!"

They probably would have arrived at that conclusion sooner had they gone in Sheni's direction rather than traipse through the jungle in the centre of the island. The entire shoreline could have only been a mile or so in circumference. Stumbling across their defunct submersible again ten minutes after setting off would have been a dead giveaway they were walking in a circle. Even from up on the tor, there wasn't much else to see. In each direction lay more trees and then more sand. And then past that, endless ocean. Well, almost endless. Now they were up high, Sheni could just about make out a much larger land mass on the horizon. The location of the resort, most likely.

"Well, better a deserted island than a *desert* island, right? And come on, Gecki. We wouldn't be real pirates if we didn't get stranded on a distant shore at some point in our lives."

"I swear to the gods, Sheni, I'm gonna fashion a kite from your innards to flag down a passing ship..."

"So we won't be walking back to the resort any time soon, then." Xotl's arms deflated. "Oh dear. Those coconuts are looking rather tempting now, aren't they?"

"Moonshine," Alan giggled.

"...or I could roast you over a spit," Gecki continued,

marching closer to Sheni, saliva dripping off her teeth, "and use the resulting smoke stack to signal our whereabouts. That way the rest of us won't starve to death before we're rescued."

"Now, I know this might sound crazy, but hear me out." Sheni gulped and pointed past her shoulder. "Instead of turning my corpse into a distress beacon, maybe we could ask those guys for help?"

Something was skimming across the ocean about a kilometre offshore. A small skiff or schooner of some kind, maybe even a small pleasure cruiser, propelled across the waves by a thruster where a sail ought to be. The calm, blue water behind it was being transfigured into a fine streak of boiling white mist.

"Kites," Gecki snarled, pointing to the sky. *"Innards."*

"Or we could just flag them down before they miss us," Sheni suggested. "Hurry!"

He raced back down the slope. Xotl followed, cartwheeling with none of their previous trepidation, quickly picking up speed and overtaking Sheni on a runaway course for the beach. Alan hopped off the edge of the tor like a lemming and vanished into the dense bracken.

Gecki growled to herself before thundering after them with the stone-faced determination of a velociraptor on the hunt.

Going down was a lot quicker and easier than going up, even if it did result in a bruised elbow when Sheni tripped over a fallen branch and covered the next eight metres either in the air or on his backside. His three crew mates were already trying to attract the ship's attention by the time he reached the shore. Gods, he was so out of shape...

All three of them were hopping up and down and

waving. Well, Gecki and Alan were. Xotl flapped their arms back and forth but was struggling to get very far off the sand.

"Hey," Sheni screamed, rushing into the surf beside them. "Over here! Somebody help us!"

"All right," Gecki rasped. "Don't come across *too* desperate."

"I think they see us," Sheni said, glancing back at them. "Yeah, they're turning this way!"

The boat – definitely a skiff, now Sheni could see it more clearly – had altered its trajectory slightly, as if planning to perform a fly-by of the island. It wasn't the fanciest ship he'd ever seen, but right then he would have accepted a leaky canoe if one had been offered. As it got closer, Sheni noticed it wasn't so much sailing the water as soaring a couple of metres above it.

"Something ain't right," Gecki rasped. "Where have we seen that ship before...?"

"Oh dear," Xotl replied, taking a couple of cautious steps backward. "Perhaps we would have been better off turning the submersible into a raft and sailing it back to land..."

"And you didn't think of that sooner?" Sheni raised his hand to shield his eyes from the sun. "Guys, what's the problem?"

The skiff roared along the shoreline, a black silhouette against the glinting reflections on the water. Everyone retreated up the beach as it drifted to a chugging stop above the lapping waves. Saltwater evaporated and a patch of sand behind its thruster began to vitrify.

"Ah."

A dark figure emerged onto the top deck of the skiff, then jumped down. She wore a black spacer jacket, and the numerous gold and silver rings pierced through the bony ridges of her skull jingled merrily as her leather boots slammed deep into the sand.

"Why, ain't this a fine coincidence?" the boss of the poachers said with a self-satisfied grin. "Looks like someone's in need of a ride. Well, climb on board, guys – *we owe you.*"

S heni didn't even bother trying to wriggle out of his restraints. The ropes binding his wrists and chest were wrapped so tight he could barely speak, and even if he somehow broke out – where, on a busted old skiff like this, was he supposed to go?

Gecki wasn't so consigned to her fate. She'd managed to saw through the ropes around her wrists easily enough. The poachers hadn't considered the sharpness of the reptile's claws. But she couldn't reach the ropes tying the four of them together. All she'd managed thus far was to give Sheni a nasty poke in the back.

"Will you stop that?" Sheni snapped. "It's bad enough pricking me. If you scratch Xotl by mistake, their enviro-suit will rupture like a deflating balloon."

"I suppose I should be grateful the poachers didn't bind *my* arms together," Xotl spluttered. "I'd be folded over like a clam."

Gecki snarled to herself and stopped jostling about. The four of them sat back-to-back, bound together by their ropes, down in the skiff's hold. Well, three of them sat. Alan dangled from his restraints with his feet a few inches off the floor, the tightness of the rope squeezing him into the shape of a kidney bean. Technically they could have tried standing up and shuffling about as one, but as Sheni had been keen to point out, there was nowhere to go. The doors were locked, as were the large hatches leading to the top deck.

Nobody was watching them. But they weren't totally alone, either.

Occupying the rest of the dingy, rusty hold was the massive corpse of a flying squid. *Mesonychoteuthis exocoetus,* as the concierge Mr. Zelewyn had called them. It was too big to fit in the hold lengthways, so most of its arms and tentacles were folded back over itself. Water still trickled down its pale, purple flesh. So did blood. There was a deep puncture hole in the squid's mantle where the harpoon had struck. Its yellow-ringed eye stared back at them blankly.

The smell was freakin' awful. Like, well... like raw fish left out to dry in the sun.

"Do you reckon they're gonna kill us?" Sheni whispered to Gecki. "An eye for an eye, you know? We did take out a couple of their guys back on the yacht."

"I would say it's a distinct possibility," Gecki rasped. "This lot ain't exactly got any quibbles about slaughtering whatever they like."

"Then why didn't the boss lady just leave us behind on that island to die? Or, you know, slit our throats right there and then on the beach?"

"I dunno, Sheni. Maybe the 'boss lady' has her own boss to deal with. Maybe she has other plans for us. Or maybe she just wants to watch us writhe about in discomfort. Sitting here speculating ain't gonna make much difference to the outcome, is it?"

"Will the two of you shut up for a moment?" Xotl sluttered. "I think I hear somebody coming!"

Sheni closed his mouth and listened. All he could make out was the sound of poachers walking back and forth across the giant grated hatch in the ceiling. It struck him as unlikely that a starfish without external auricles would have a better sense of hearing than him, but, sure enough, heavy footsteps stomped down the stairwell outside the hold. A weighty handle was wrenched to one side and the metal door across from them creaked open.

The boss of the poachers marched in, saw them tied up in the corner, and broke into a wide, incredulous smile.

"Hey, I almost forgot you lot were down here. Been having quite the celebration up top." She jabbed a thumb behind her at the dead squid. "Caught two of these monsters this time."

"How impressive," Sheni replied bitterly. "Slaughtering rare animals. *Very* noble."

"Yeah, well, it helps to not have a bunch of killers around to mess up your plans. What are you, spacers? Pirates?"

"Something like that," Gecki rasped. "We're retired."

"Oh, I bet you are." The boss brought her face close to Gecki's. Not *too* close, though. "Did Nova Elysia hire you to run security on their yacht, or something?"

"No. Like I said, we're *retired*. That means we don't work, get it?"

"We're guests at the resort," Sheni grumbled. "Same as all the others on that boat. Just, you know, a bit less fanciful."

"Well I never." The boss stood up straight and stepped back to take a better look at them. She put her hands on her hips. "Ex-pirates rich enough to splash credits on pedicures and drinks with little fruits on the rim. Looks like I picked the wrong line of work, right?"

"Clearly," Xotl replied in their deadpan tone, "given that your career involves killing defenceless animals."

"Look, lady." Gecki flexed her neck. "What do you want from us, huh? We're sorry about your crew. You know, the ones we offed on the yacht. But we were just defending ourselves, same as you would have done. So captain to captain, why don't you just let us go, yeah?"

The boss stared at them, still smiling, her mouth twisted up at one side as if she were digging something out from between her teeth with her tongue. Gods, she had to be hot in that leather jacket of hers. Sheni wondered if Kerulians could regulate their temperature better than humans. Maybe she'd just grown up on a world hotter than this.

"Hey, Sylva," said a scrawny insectoid lurking inside the door to the stairwell. "Just a heads up. We're less than ten minutes out."

"I hear ya, Cragg. Be up in just a moment."

Sylva waited until her subordinate had scampered back upstairs before returning her attention to her captives, that same twisted smile still etched across a face heavy with gold and silver rings.

"Nash and Bort were good lads. Not the smartest pair, but they worked hard and got the job done. I ain't exactly best pleased with you killing them, so nah, I ain't letting you four go so easily. Specially not considering all the valuables we could have looted from that fancy yacht of yours."

"So, what?" Sheni nodded past Sylva. "We gonna end up like our squid friend over there, is that what you're saying?"

"Maybe. Maybe not." Sylva crossed her arms. "If you were just a bunch of scraggly nobodies, I'd pilfer what you had on your persons right now and then chuck your corpses in the ocean. But now I know you're loaded... well, that changes everything, don't it?"

"Yeah, that does seem to be the case," Sheni sighed.

"What's ten minutes out?" Gecki snarled, tilting her snout up to the boots clanging against the grates above their heads.

"Base camp," Sylva replied. "Gotta offload this cargo and get ready for the next run. I'll decide what to do with you there. Fortunately for you, I'm a pragmatic woman. Figure we can still turn a profit if we ransom you off."

Sheni groaned. He just wanted to go back to the resort, drown himself in foreign beer and pretend like this whole day had never happened.

"You're barking up the wrong tree, lady. There's nobody out there willing to—"

Gecki jabbed Sheni in the back with her claw.

"Oh, yeah," Sheni said, wincing as he figuratively swerved to avoid a death sentence. "We've got *loads* of friends back home. Too many, if anything. Can barely even remember their names. I'm sure *one* of them will be willing to pay for our safe return, right?"

"*Safe* return," Gecki stressed. "Not in sixteen different parcels, you hear me?"

"Dismantled deliverables," Alan cooed softly, eyes bulging as the rope squeezed deeper into what amounted to the green ball's waist.

Sylva laughed and scratched at her skull-feathers.

"Yeah, yeah. Sure. Whatever. Nobody pays up, we take all your crap, then kill you. And hey, maybe we'll kill you even if somebody *does* pay your ransom. Be kinda fun, won't it?"

"Oh, yeah. Sounds like a real blast," Sheni said. "Here's a

thought. How about you take us back to the resort and *we'll* pay the ransom? Cut out the middle man, you know?"

"And have you run screaming to the authorities the second we get there?" Sylva gave him a pitying look. "Nah, friend. You're sticking with us. And after you've seen our hideout, you ain't going *nowhere*. Least not till we're done."

Sheni lowered his head and found his mouth too dry to swallow. Done? Done with what? The poaching, or with them?

"Right, I'd better get upstairs." Sylva clapped her hands together, barked out another sharp laugh and half-skipped back to the stairwell. "Don't want the goons sailing this skiff all the way up the shore and into the trees, do we? Sit tight, friends. Won't be long now."

She slammed the door shut behind her. Nobody said anything for a while, just marinated in the stench of dead mollusc.

"This is not turning out to be a very relaxing vacation," Xotl spluttered.

"How long until we're like our squid friend over there, do you reckon?" Sheni asked. "One day? Two?"

"Oh, I'd give us a few hours at best," Gecki rasped. "They'll gut us the second they realise we ain't got any rich friends to pay that ransom they're after."

"We barely have any friends, full stop," Xotl added despondently.

"Hey, let's not be too negative." Sheni twisted around to look at Gecki and Xotl in turn. "The Ministry's on the hunt for these poachers, right? Maybe they'll show up and rescue us..."

Silence fell over them again, heavy as a wet blanket. Then Gecki resumed furiously hacking at their ropes.

"We're gonna make our own escape," she snarled, "coz I ain't becoming somebody's handbag."

CHAPTER
ELEVEN

The skiff chugged and grunted to a hesitant stop. Three poachers, one of whom was the insectoid individual Sylva had referred to as Cragg, came down to the hold to collect the crew of the *Silver Hart*. The ropes binding them together remained tightly wrapped around their waists.

Sheni winced as they emerged onto the top deck. The sun remained painfully high and bright in the sky; he estimated it wasn't long past midday. His group was pushed and shoved across the creaking wooden boards, past the rapidly cooling thruster, over the iron grate under which the squid's body lay, and down a rickety ramp leading onto yet another pink-sanded beach.

This one wasn't quite as tranquil as the beach they'd had to themselves back on the deserted island.

A large swathe of trees had been cut back to make room for the poachers' camp, and the lumber used to erect temporary structures in which they slept, ate and prepared the poached animals to be shipped off-world. In the shaded workshop of one such building, a butcher hacked at assorted chunks of squid. Plastic refrigeration crates were stacked high on the boarded promenade outside, ready for transportation. Unlike a pirate camp, the rest of the occupants weren't just sitting around and drinking. The poachers – those not disembarking the skiff alongside Sheni and his crew – were busy getting a second ship stocked and repaired for the next hunting party.

Sheni, Gecki, Xotl and Alan – who still dangled like a squeezed lime, pinned to the others by the tautness of the rope – were forced to waddle up the shore. A few of the poachers stopped what they were doing to laugh. As much as Sheni wanted to punch the smiles off their faces, he couldn't exactly blame them. Under less perilous circumstances, he reckoned he would have found the sight of them hogtied together kind of funny, too.

Behind them, a crane – also built largely using resources torn from the jungle – lifted the dead squid from the cargo hold of Sylva's skiff. The wooden struts creaked ominously with the creature's weight, and Sheni was sure the squid would slip out of the leathery harness strapped around its mantle, but it slowly made its precarious journey above everyone's heads intact.

This was a professional poaching outfit, Sheni conceded, not some opportunistic band of raiders. They might be scrappy and cheap, but only with the purpose of maximising profit. Sylva knew exactly what she was doing.

"Lock these troublemakers up," Sylva ordered, disembarking the skiff as the squid was lowered onto a platform further down the boardwalk. "We'll get this bad boy prepped for dissection and then decide what we do with them."

"Dissection, yeah?" Cragg nudged them forward with

the butt of his shoddy plasma rifle. "That sound good to you?"

The crew said nothing. They obediently shuffled past the wooden shacks to a bunch of cages at the rear of the camp, half-hidden by luscious ferns. They were built from hardened bamboo wrapped in rope and a few had wild animals trapped inside. Cragg told them to stop and then opened the door to a larger cage, about two metres cubed, before ordering them inside.

"I'm surprised you ain't more on board with all this," Cragg said, one hand on the door, "what with you four being pirates and all."

"We're nothing alike," Gecki snarled as they ducked into the cage.

"If you say so," Cragg replied. "You kill, we kill. Same difference."

"We've done bad things, sure. Stole a bunch and yeah, killed a person or two. But they're *people*. They had it coming, most of the time. You lot target animals who can't properly defend themselves, wipe out whole ecosystems for a quick credit. You're scum, that's what you are. *Scum*."

"Yeah. Well." Cragg slammed the barred door shut. "I ain't the one in a cage."

He inserted a wooden plank across the door like a drawbar to keep it from swinging outward – the DIY cage didn't possess a lock – then marched off back to camp. The crew waited a few seconds, checked that nobody was paying them any attention, and then dropped the rope binding them together.

"Nice work, everyone," Sheni whispered. "Gecki, well done for not flipping out and slashing the throat of everyone in sight."

"It took a lot of restraint," she grumbled. "Let's figure a way out of this cage before I change my mind."

Gecki tried reaching through the bars to remove the plank blocking the door, but she couldn't quite reach. She stepped back to let Sheni have a go. His arms were slightly thinner. But he couldn't get to it, either.

"Alan," he whispered. "Do you think you can squeeze through the bars and unlock the door from outside?"

Their diminutive companion stumbled from gangly foot to gangly foot, his eyes rolling even more waywardly than usual, his body still bent in the middle where the rope had dug in. Alan hiccuped, giggled, and then sat down hard on his backside.

"Oh dear," Xotl sighed. "I believe we have broken Alan."

"But he's all bent out of shape," Gecki rasped. "It's the best time to push him through!"

"Erm, guys?" Sheni nodded past the dense ferns toward the camp. "Not that we shouldn't be concerned about Alan's lack of elasticity, but I think Sylva and the gang have some company..."

Commotion consumed the hideout. A lot of the poachers were rushing from cabin to cabin and grabbing rifles, but Sylva remained perfectly calm, as if the visitors were expected. Gecki joined Sheni and pressed her snout through the door.

"Is it the Plillup guards from Porto Kumasa?" she asked. "Gods, I never thought I'd be glad to see *their* faces again."

"Not unless those fish people have started driving all-terrain vehicles..."

Two black trucks, each sporting six wheels and enough reinforced panelling on their chassis to knock down half the trees in the jungle, rumbled into camp, their tyres crunching to a stop on the baking sand. Unlike the poachers, these people had credits. *Real* credits. Each of those trucks probably cost as much as the *Silver Hart*. A green stripe ran down their flanks, a twin-rack of high-intensity light bars was installed above the windscreen and front grille, and all the windows were tinted a dark maroon colour.

A pair of guards stepped out from the cabin of the truck closest to the cage. Each carried a sleek, militaristic rifle. A third guard climbed down from the driver's seat of the second truck. They stood a good half a dozen metres away from Sylva and her crew, their rifles pointed down at the ground, yet still very much standing to attention.

"What in the galaxy is happening out there?" Xotl asked, poking an eye-dotted arm past Sheni. "Oh, I do hope nobody starts shooting. I thought I was done with that nonsense."

A fourth individual – a Qualian, Sheni reckoned – exited the second truck and stalked over to Sylva. Sheni squinted past the ferns, but he couldn't get a good look at them. They were wearing a lot of copper beads, that's all he could tell. It was only when Sylva greeted them that the pieces fell into place.

"Mr. Zelewyn," she said, crossing her arms. "Wasn't expecting you today."

Sheni turned to Gecki, open mouthed and appalled. Gecki sniffed the air in irritation. Why was the hotel manager of the Nova Elysia consorting with a bunch of bloodthirsty poachers?

"I'm sure you weren't, Ms. Sylva, but then again I wasn't expecting my resort's yacht to be attacked by your men yesterday, was I? Perhaps I was foolish to think you could handle an operation of this magnitude."

"I had no idea the yacht was yours. And I didn't tell

those two idiots to attack it, either," she lied. Sheni had seen her scowling at them from the skiff they used to board it. "Anyways, the culprits responsible were swiftly dealt with by those guests of yours, weren't they? I can assure you it won't happen again."

"It had better not. Please keep your crew in check, Ms. Sylva. That little episode caused quite the stir at the resort. I had to pull a number of strings to keep the Ministerium from getting involved. Not that I expect you to appreciate the delicate balance of diplomacy."

"It won't happen again," Sylva repeated, this time more stonily, the twisted smirk vanishing from her face. "Take a look at this beauty. Dragged him from the waters not one hour ago."

Mr. Zelewyn took a graceful step forward, finally coming into Sheni's view. He didn't look particularly vexed that he had to deal with a cutthroat criminal like Sylva. Then again, it was hard to tell with Qualians. They were infuriatingly cordial to everybody, even their mortal enemies. Not that their species made many of those, mind.

"Why would I be impressed by this?" he asked, turning his question mark-shaped body away from the dead squid being gently lowered onto the platform. Even this furious retort came across as insufferably polite. "Slaughtering the flying squid was never the end goal, only the means. An end you seem no closer to reaching, may I add."

"Yeah, but the means comes *before* the end. That's how it works." Sylva gave Zelewyn a mocking look. "And we're poachers – you do realise that, right? It's kinda what we do."

"Then perhaps you should aspire to be more. We had a deal. If you can't make good on our arrangement, I'm sure the Ministerium will be extremely interested in hearing about the little operation you have going on here."

"Yeah, yeah. Calm your giblets, boss. These things don't happen overnight. Just give us a bit more time, got it?"

The smirk was back. Sylva's goons glanced at each other and snickered. Mr. Zelewyn and his armed guards remained emotionless, though without facial features Zelewyn didn't exactly have many options in that department.

Sheni elbowed Gecki and whispered, "What on earth is going on here?"

"Don't know, don't care." She scratched the scales under her chin. "You reckon Mr. Zelewyn would take us back to the resort if we called out to him?"

"No, Gecki. After what we've seen, I reckon he'd tell Sylva to make sure we never get out of this cage alive!"

Behind them, having regained much of his original shape, Alan gurgled incomprehensibly and shuffled through the bars of their cage, disappearing into the jungle foliage.

"Good grief," Sheni sighed. "All he had to do was open the freakin' door..."

Mr. Zelewyn, after a long time spent studying the poachers with the fleshy lump he called a head, waved a graceful hand at one of his guards, who marched to the back of one of their trucks and returned carrying a large crate. The guard dropped it onto the sand in front of Sylva and popped open the lid.

"What have we here?" Sylva cooed, her eyes lighting up. "All this for me? Shucks, you daft Qualian. You shouldn't have."

"Explosive charges from the resort's original construction," Mr. Zelewyn kindly explained. "Your approach isn't working, Ms. Sylva. Killing their squid only strengthens the Plillup of Porto Kumasa's resolve. Blow up their home. If they won't depart of their own accord, leave them no other choice."

"And then?" she asked, running her tongue over her teeth as she plucked an explosive from the crate. "When the job is done?"

"You will receive payment as promised," Mr. Zelewyn replied, "and you and your crew shall vacate these waters for good."

Sheni couldn't believe what he was overhearing. Zelewyn came across like such a lovely hotel concierge, always checking on everyone's wellbeing and organising embarrassing dance parties and making sure the elderly guests knew to take the shortcut between the mud pools and the sauna hut, lest they find themselves trapped in the lazy river. Yet here he was, instructing a bunch of career criminals to destroy a protected underwater settlement. It didn't make any sense. There had to be some kind of misunderstanding, some aspect of the deal Sheni was missing.

Mr. Zelewyn bowed elegantly, and then he and his guards returned to their trucks. Their engines ignited one after the other in short succession. Alan burst up from the ferns perfectly in time with the second mechanical roar and beckoned for them to follow with his weedy green finger.

"Hey, Alan's back," Sheni gasped, nudging Gecki. "Did you find a way out of here, man?"

"You did, didn't you?" Gecki rasped, clutching the bars. "No, stop waving at us and come get the freakin' door..."

Cragg strolled to the back of the camp about thirty seconds later, shaking his head and listening to the grumble of the trucks as they bulldozed their way back into the jungle. He leaned against the cage and smirked to himself.

"You catch much of that?" he asked the crew, staring

down the shoreline. "Bet you feel stupid now, don't ya, protecting that swanky yacht full of—"

He glanced casually into the cage, then jumped, goosebumps breaking out across his whole body. Its only occupant was a long, frayed coil of rope.

"Ah, nuts. Sylva's gonna be pissed..."

CHAPTER
TWELVE

A set of gates hidden toward the rear of the Nova Elysia resort automatically rumbled open upon the two trucks' approach. The road beyond wound deep into the jungle, eventually connecting the resort with the nearest town two dozen kilometres further up the coast. The trucks pulled into a pair of bays under the concrete awning of a loading dock and the drivers killed the engines.

Mr. Zelewyn gracefully stepped down from the passenger-side door of one cabin, straightened out the beads dangling over his curved chest, and then glided off in the direction of the guest areas. The three guards who'd accompanied him to Sylva's hideout also disembarked and left the barren yard, returning to either their regular posts or the resort's security offices.

Nothing stirred in the loading dock except for a pterosaur cawing in the sky and a leaf falling from a tree that had dared extend a branch over the resort's tall perimeter wall.

Then the rear door of the left-hand truck creaked open and a human face poked out.

"Looks clear," Sheni whispered. "Let's hope nobody in the back office is watching the exterior cameras too closely..."

"Unless you want to spend the rest of your life trapped in this stuffy box," Gecki rasped, "we ain't got much of a choice. Go on, get out."

Sheni hopped down, then Gecki, and then the two of them helped lower Xotl and Alan to the concrete floor. Gecki peered around the side of the truck while Sheni quietly locked the door behind them.

"Nice work getting us out of that poacher camp, Alan," he whispered. "I think somebody's earned themselves a kwagua juice."

Alan blinked happily, having returned to his rotund shape during their short road trip.

"Yes, yes, very good," Gecki rasped. "Can we focus on finding our way back to safety, please?"

"Don't you think we should stop and talk about what we just witnessed?" Sheni asked.

"Sure, yeah. But maybe not in the staff-only area of a luxury resort run by the dodgy guy we're chatting about, huh?"

"The conversation would certainly be easier paired with a coconut spritz or two," Xotl said enthusiastically. "I dare say we've earned it after the day we've had."

"Don't worry so much. Mr. Zelewyn has no idea we were in Sylva's camp. If a guard catches us in an off-limits section, we'll just tell them we got lost."

"'Lost' won't get me a steak sandwich, Sheni. I'm starving."

"How can you be hungry right now, Gecki?"

"I guess I just worry better on a full stomach," she replied, shrugging sarcastically. "Now shut up and follow me, all right?"

They sneaked around the truck and up the steps of the loading dock. Past a pair of forcefields was the warehouse, its enormous shelves no doubt stocked full of expensive ingredients, drinks and spare pillows. Sheni suspected that stepping through the hard blue light without the right biometrics would be a mistake. If they were lucky an alarm would go off. If they were unlucky, not every piece of them would reach the other side...

Fortunately, there was a reassuringly boring-looking door a little further on. They crept down the platform toward it, sticking to the shadowy wall.

"What happens if it's locked?" Sheni asked. "Reckon we should knock?"

"Nah," Gecki rasped. "We climb over the rear gate and sneak around the wall to the front of the resort. The guards there will recognise us as guests and let us stroll in, no problem."

"Won't they wonder what we're doing out in the jungle?"

"Ah, we're rich. Confidently wandering into dangerous territory for no discernible reason is the kind of stupid thing they expect us to do."

Luckily, the door wasn't locked. Sheni wondered if it had something to do with their IDs being scanned automatically, like back when he'd tried to pay for the submersible, or if the security systems hadn't reset since the armed guards returned from their visit to Sylva's camp. If it was the former, they could probably expect their presence to be logged somewhere. Oh well. They were guests at the Nova Elysia. The worst punishment on the cards was being asked to leave without getting their deposit back.

It *was* a pretty big deposit, though.

The staff corridors were nothing like as fancy as those witnessed by the guests, but they were still in substantially better condition than the corridors of the few hotels Sheni had stayed at in his life, let alone anywhere on ramshackle space stations such as the Corpse & Casket. They were plain, painted in simple whites and creams, with arrows pointing employees in the direction of the resort's various facilities. The quicker staff could get where they needed to go, the better the experience for the guests. That's how Sheni interpreted the dull, corporate blandness, anyway.

"Pool Foyer," Xotl spluttered, reading one of the signs painted on the wall at the next junction. "That seems like a sensible enough place to go, doesn't it?"

"Better than Laundry," Gecki replied, checking the other signs. "And a lot closer than the Main Foyer, I expect. And the sooner we get somewhere we ought to be, the more plausible Sheni's idea of claiming we got lost becomes, you know?"

"See?" he whispered. "I'm not always an idiot."

"Nah, but you sure get your idiocy in early, don't you?"

"What does that even mean, Gecki?"

"Ah, I see you keep *some* stupidity in reserve."

"Can the two of you stop bickering and focus?" Xotl asked. Their arms wilted. "Alan's already halfway to the ice cream buffet."

They followed their wayward friend down the corridor toward the Pool Foyer, past the unmarked doors of closets and offices. Sheni saw palm trees and artificial waterfalls outside the window. Back to normality. Thank goodness. He didn't care how fake it was. Fake was safe.

A Qualian suddenly glided through a set of doors at the far end of the corridor, a bundle of greasy French fry baskets in his slender arms, but he was too immersed in his work to turn his fleshy stump of a head in the crew's direction. They waited until he disappeared through the doors of the nearby waste recycling room and then exited the way he came.

"Ah," Sheni sighed as they swapped chilly climate-controlled air for the roasting heat of a tropical paradise. "That's more like it."

They were standing beneath the domed ceiling of a marble bandstand flanked by spiralling pillars and purple and pink flower petals. To their left, cascading terraces of mud pools in which the families of more elephantine guests – such as the Alpha Rhoden – soaked and caked in the sun. To their right, a heated swimming pool featuring the two-storey artificial waterfall Sheni spotted through the window earlier, plus an archway of water fountains. And in between, a well-stocked swim-up bar accommodating both. The odours of sugary drinks and triple-fried snacks wafted over them as gently as the pulsating Qualian pop music.

"And not a moment too godsdamn soon," Gecki rasped, sniffing the air. "I'm famished. Look, my scales are practically hanging off me. I doubt there are tables available at diCarsko's at this short notice, but the Pearl Lounge can probably rustle up a seafood platter or two."

"Hold on, are you forgetting something? We have the small matter of a genocide to sort out."

"Sure, but we ain't stopping nothing while my stomach's growling like a Krolak."

"Then grab a freakin' bagel on the way, or something! If we don't confront Mr. Zelewyn, or call up the Ministry, or at least do *something* to understand what the hell's going on here, innocent people are gonna die!"

Gecki rolled her eye and placed a heavy hand on Sheni's shoulder.

"Innocent people are *always* gonna die, Sheni. It's a fact of life, plain and simple. Like I asked you last night, what do you think *we* can do to stop it? Call up the Ministry if you think it'll make any difference. It sounds like Mr. Zelewyn already has them in his pocket."

"We can find out why—"

"Sheni, *listen to me.*" Her grip on his shoulder tightened. "We went down to Porto Kumasa and we almost died. We got captured by Sylva and her crew of poachers and *we almost died*. We're spacers on vacation, not intergalactic peacekeepers. Can you wrap your simian brain around that? It's not our problem, and there's nothing we can do to help. Let the professionals deal with this. Or not. They're the ones who'll have to answer for it either way."

Sheni pulled away from Gecki and threw his hands in the air in frustration.

"Come on, Xotl. Back me up. You think we should help these people, right?"

Xotl folded onto the floor in shame.

"I feel bad knowing what awaits those poor Plillup," they spluttered, "but I have to say I agree with Gecki on this occasion. We simply aren't equipped to stop the poachers. Perhaps it would be best to send the Ministerium a message and then get on with the rest of our holiday."

"I can't believe I'm hearing this." Sheni put his hands on his hips. "Alan would be on board with this if he knew what was going on."

"I think Alan just wants an ice cream," Gecki rasped, breaking into a sinister grin as Alan excitedly waggled his gangly arms above his head.

"Fine. Whatever." Sheni sagged and groaned. "You go and get fat on free lobsters if you want. I can't be that heartless."

"I get it." Gecki's tired but not altogether unkind sigh felt like the epilogue to their argument. "You're a good guy, Sheni. You don't like it when other good people get hurt. But you ain't a hero. None of us are. And it ain't any of our business. If you hadn't insisted on breaking the rules to go visit them, we wouldn't even know the Plillup were in danger, would we?"

She winced at a sharp crick in her neck and turned her scaly snout in the direction of sizzling meat skewers. Clouds of steam rose above the swim-up bar.

"Now that's settled, let's eat. Barbecue sounds good, right? And then we hit the spa. I don't know about you, but my shoulders could *really* do with a massage."

Gecki unlocked the door to her hotel room and stomped inside, relishing the swampy humidity that rushed forth to welcome her.

Well, that could have gone better.

Sheni was so hung up on doing the 'right thing', he rarely stopped to consider what the right thing actually was. And for whom. And *why*. As far as he seemed concerned, if something seemed nice, it therefore was – consequences be damned.

She'd thought their little argument had been the end of it. So imagine her surprise when instead of following her to the barbecue sizzling away behind the swim-up bar like a sensible person, Sheni had stormed off in the direction of the Main Foyer, way on the other side of the resort. Xotl had deflated and spluttered something about needing a stiff drink before cartwheeling away across the hot tiles. And when she'd looked back down at her clawed feet, Alan had vanished, too.

So much for crew solidarity. That's what all this was about, wasn't it? Keeping her crew together. Keeping her crew safe. Gecki didn't care what Sheni thought or felt about the dumb Plillup situation. She just wanted to make sure he didn't run off on his own and get himself killed.

But the idiot was gonna end up drowned, eaten or shot, anyway. She wished she could put a leash on him like they talked about doing with Alan sometimes, but apparently the Ministry frowned upon that sort of thing, even when it came to humans.

Gecki slinked across the room, spinning the dial of the thermostat toward maximum humidity as she passed it, and jabbed a claw at the screen on the wall. It had been showing a rolling feed of amenities available to guests but now displayed a catalogue of beverage options. The dispenser mounted beside it gurgled out the booze she'd requested. She growled irritably and the machine made it a double.

Past the enormous circular bed covered in crumpled purple sheets – as per her request when booking the room – Gecki curled up in the groove of a bronze chair shaped like an upright horseshoe in the corner of her balcony. The privacy bubble was still closed – she didn't want to let any of the steam out, obviously – but if she wiped the glass she could see right the way down to the myriad amoeba-shaped pools below.

Children splashing about, riding waterslides, screaming and having fun.

Gods, it was intolerable.

Gecki sipped her drink and tried to get comfortable in the chair. It wasn't easy. Everything in the resort was so over-produced, so artistic and bespoke, you'd think the furniture's sole purpose was to *look* nice, not feel nice...

Oh no. She was starting to think like Sheni.

Forty years she'd been a spacer, a pirate, a dirty rotten scoundrel tearing from star system to star system. Forty years. Almost three quarters of her life, up until now. And in that time she'd clawed and stabbed and scraped credits together just to get by, to make a life for herself, to become somebody whose name would be remembered after she was gone.

There were two end goals for a pirate: either to become the top dog, a Dread Pirate King or Queen if you had truly delusional aspirations, or to get out of the game with your pockets full and your head still attached to your neck. Most other finish lines were marked with a tombstone.

Honestly, she'd settle for the second option. People knew her (and yes, by extension Sheni and Xotl and Alan) as the captain who discovered the legendary Sword of Bokata. She was richer than she ever *really* believed a lizard like her could be. And what's more, she'd *earned* it. Over the years they'd battled snowstorms, escaped Ministerium prisons, defended Kapamentis against the ancient Prymalis fleet. Hell, they'd almost lost their lives stealing a priceless egg – *twice!* Didn't they deserve to relax, put their feet up and ignore all the awful crap in which the rest of the galaxy wallowed, just for once?

Gecki gave up trying to get comfortable and downed the rest of her drink in one. She'd come upstairs to clear her head, maybe soak in the tub a while, but now she was alone in her room, she just felt like she wasn't making the most of her time at Nova Elysia. Sitting at the bar by herself didn't sound all that inviting, though. Neither did basking on the sand. Besides, all the cabanas would be taken by now.

She could try and find Xotl, she supposed. Make sure they were doing all right. Piece the crew back together from there.

Or maybe she had a better idea.

"Time to hit the beauty salon," she rasped triumphantly

to herself, as she flexed her sore shoulders. "You know what they say, Gecki. You can't care for others until you first take care of yourself."

S heni marched down the corridors of the resort with a scowl on his face, much to the confusion of the Qualian staff members he crossed paths with. They'd never seen a guest look so disappointed before. Not in Nova Elysia.

"Stupid reptile," he muttered. "Only thinks about herself. Won't get up off her scaly arse unless she thinks credits are involved. She wouldn't even *be* in this freakin' resort if I hadn't insisted on finding that damn sword."

"Can I interest you in a complementary sweet roll?" one of the attendants asked. She was pushing a hover-cart piled high with cinnamon and sugar. "Freshly baked on-site, we delight ourselves on—"

"Yes, you can," Sheni snapped, grumpily snatching up a *kanelbulle*. "Thank you. I'm sure it's absolutely lovely."

He ate it on the move. Yes, it was delicious. Yes, the flakes melted like buttery snowflakes on his tongue. Having grown up in France, even one beset by riots during the collapse of civilisation, he knew a thing or two about good pastries. But the flurry of flavour still wasn't enough to douse his bitterness.

"An entire Plillup community is at risk of being blown up," he grumbled to himself, "and all that dumb lizard can think about is booking herself in for a *shoulder rub*? Stars above…"

Sheni finally reached the Main Foyer. He hadn't visited this part of the resort since first arriving at Nova Elysia a few days ago. The front entrance was a wide, elongated archway of pure gold. Outside that, a spectacular water feature boasted leaping fountains and rare orange and yellow fish. A well-trimmed path of grass wound through the trees to the spaceport hidden two miles further inland – far enough away to mask the worst of the thruster-roar from the ships that came and went. That's where the *Silver Hart* was presently parked. There were armed guards on constant watch, but they kept themselves concealed amongst the ferns for the most part, unlike the Qualian concierges who made themselves almost overwhelmingly visible to everyone arriving.

Inside was no less breathtaking. Eight receptionists – five Qualians, two Oortilians and a bug-eyed Drosophike – worked behind a front desk that followed the curvature of the foyer's wall. Realistic holograms of waterfalls, meteorite showers and schools of fish danced high on the domed ceiling. Flower displays flanked petite boutiques. The air smelled of cinnamon – from the bakery, Sheni guessed – and lavender. A four-armed Krolak sat on a stage playing a complicated hand-drum instrument arranged in a full circle around her person, each hit soft and slightly melancholy to Sheni's ears, while around her guests drank their welcome drinks, waited for their luggage to be brought up to their rooms, and excitedly discussed which of the resort's renowned amenities they'd sample first.

None of the staff had swooped down on him yet, but Sheni knew it was only a matter of time once all the new arrivals were dealt with.

He'd rather they didn't. Everyone here was so keen to help, but Sheni doubted they'd tell him where Mr. Zelewyn's private office was if he asked.

Presumably it was nearby, though. It made sense, right?

Most of the issues and disagreements in a hotel happened down at the front desk, when rooms weren't up to snuff or prices weren't as expected or somebody couldn't work the thermostat. A manager like Mr. Zelewyn needed to be close by in order to step in and remedy the situation. Sheni couldn't imagine problems like that happening often in Nova Elysia, but still. You can build the best resort in the galaxy, but you can't make the guests any less difficult.

Take him, for example. He was having a lovely time at the resort – while he was in it, at any rate – and *still* he had the nerve to take issue with the hotel manager employing a bunch of poachers to wipe out a protected settlement.

You just can't please some people.

Sheni searched for a door or a forcefield barrier leading to the management offices, or whatever equivalent Qualian infrastructure possessed. He spotted a staff-only door behind the front desk, and he imagined that would take him where he wanted to go eventually, but it was useless. No way were any of those receptionists going to let him through, with or without an escort.

He left the Main Foyer via another of its archways and followed a path cast in the shade of enormous palm trees. It ran almost parallel with the exterior of a building connected to the foyer, though this one was mostly disguised by its green walls and intentionally placed vines. Definitely off-limits to guests, just like the bland corridors the crew had wandered down not half an hour earlier. He could tell because pretty much every other building in the resort was designed to be as ostentatious and easy to access as possible.

Turning right at the next fork in the path, he discovered a double door on automatic piston-hinges, practically buried behind a wall of climbing hydrangeas. They didn't open as Sheni approached. This didn't surprise him. His biometrics were supposed to only permit him access to guest facilities. But even if he kept following the building around, which would likely involve traipsing through the nice flowerbeds, he doubted any other entrances were less guarded or conspicuous.

A pair of Mansa aristocrats took the other path at the fork and walked past Sheni without so much as a glance in his direction. He reckoned he was pretty well concealed back here. All he needed to do was hide and wait for somebody to exit the office, then dart in before the door closed again. Hopefully without setting off any kind of alert in the process.

He leaned against the green wall and waited.

Twenty minutes must have passed without so much as a dragonfly buzzing in his vicinity. Sheni started to think this doorway was another relic from the resort's construction, perhaps, just like the explosives now in Sylva's possession – that it led down to a half-abandoned sub-basement and nobody actually used it anymore. But then the pistons hissed and the doors opened with an electronic beep. Sheni quickly darted behind a large fern to keep from being spotted.

An attendant walked outside, their bare feet scarcely touching the path, dressed in the black Qualian equivalent of a chef's uniform. They passed Sheni and continued down the path, presumably in the direction of the restaurant quarter. Sheni waited for as long as he dared and then scurried inside just as the doors were starting to shut.

"Okay," he mumbled to himself. "Now to find out where Mr. Zelewyn does his paperwork."

Sheni was no idiot, no matter what Gecki said. He knew that if he called up the Ministry or the local Queflian authorities and told them the manager of the Nova Elysia resort had hired poachers to blow up Porto Kumasa, they'd laugh him off the planet. The idea was preposterous. Even Sheni wasn't sure he believed it. That's why he needed evidence. There had to be something in all these admin offices that tied Zelewyn to Sylva. And even if the evidence wasn't enough to get the Ministry to take him seriously, he had to do *something*, didn't he? He'd never be able to lie down on a sun lounger and enjoy his rum punch otherwise.

Evidently those working in Resort Management and Administration were treated to fancier workspaces than those replenishing towel stock and shepherding desserts from one sector to another. Here the walls were painted serene blues and decorated with abstract landscapes. Ornate glow-strips bulged from the ceiling and the floors were carpeted with a plush blue wool (particularly pleasant for the Qualians' bare feet, Sheni reckoned, though likely synthetic). It wasn't a million miles away from the decor Sheni saw in the guest corridors outside his room, just with a little more focus on the practical side of things.

The reception desk in the Main Foyer had to be over to his right, so he followed the corridor left until he reached a much wider perpendicular gallery lined with tall, narrow, grey doors. A staircase that alternated direction with each flight occupied one side of the hall. A long stretch of windowless interior offices took up the rest of the floor. A Qualian electrician was standing on a hovering footstool while she fixed a light on the staircase's landing. Sheni ducked back behind the corner of the wall as three accountants emerged from one of the lofty doors and strolled toward him, discussing the resort's monthly metrics. He chewed his lip and balked at the astronomic figures they casually threw around.

Dammit. He'd rushed in without thinking things

through, as per usual. How was he supposed to find Zewelyn's office? Presuming he even had one, that is. But everyone who ran things had their own private room, didn't they? Perk of the job, you know? Still, it could be anywhere. Upstairs, downstairs, in an open plan bullpen in the core of the building. Every species envisioned corporate environments differently. Every corporation, too.

And not only did he somehow need to find Zewelyn's office *and* get inside, he needed to do so without being spotted by anyone who worked for the resort. Because something in Sheni's gut told him questions would be raised at the sight of a stray human knocking on a dozen different doors.

He waited for the three accountants to pass, then checked the corridor.

Then again, he considered, nobody who wasn't supposed to be wandering around back here would *ever* be so stupid and brash as to go up and actually speak to somebody...

Sheni hurried up the first set of steps, approached the electrician from behind, and tapped her politely on her bare shoulder.

"I'm awfully sorry," he said in his most timid and apologetic voice. "I'm supposed to have a meeting with Mr. Zelewyn in his office, but I've forgotten where it is. Us silly humans don't have great memories! I don't suppose you could point me in the right direction? I'd feel just awful if I was late. Just *awful*."

Sheni wished he could read Qualian emotions. Why their species had felt the need to evolve without visible eyes or mouths was beyond him. It made it extremely difficult to tell whether this individual was peering down at him with pity or about to scream for security.

He was hoping to appeal to their species' innate sense of politeness. To ignore a request for help from somebody who was himself so polite – such rudeness just wasn't in the average Qualian's blood.

But they were also incredibly intelligent, he remembered at the last moment. Certainly smart enough to see through one cheeky human's ruse...

"Oh, I am sure Mr. Zelewyn would be most understanding," the electrician replied, much to Sheni's relief. They raised their featureless head. "Two floors up, then take a left. The door to Mr. Zelewyn's office will be on your right. It's clearly labelled, you shouldn't miss it."

"Thank you," Sheni said brightly, almost skipping up the stairs in his excitement to leave. "I really mean it, thank you so much!"

He raced up both flights of steps, prepared to stop for no-one, then paused at the top while he waited for two members of staff – another Qualian and an insectoid Krettelian, this time – to finish chatting beside a holo-screen that was reeling off performance targets. Then he tiptoed down the corridor immediately to his left as instructed until he arrived at the door to Mr. Zelewyn's office. It looked no different from any of the others save for the name plaque installed just above Sheni's head.

Sheni tried the door. There wasn't a visible handle, so he gave it a shove.

It wouldn't budge. A hand scanner was installed just to the right of the door, and it flashed red at Sheni's attempt to get in. He gave the touch-screen a tentative prod and it flashed red again.

"Of course he locks it," Sheni muttered. "Guy's got something to hide."

He jumped as something patted his leg just below his

shorts. Alan was standing beside him and holding the largest ice cream cone Sheni had ever seen. One scoop was pink, the other orange. Both were the size of Alan's eyes and dripping onto the nice carpet.

"Oh, hey buddy. I'm glad *somebody* cares about stopping those poachers. We're wasting our time, though. Can't get inside."

Alan plunged one of his tiny hands into his ice cream, then jumped up and high-fived the scanner. It left a gloopy, strawberry-flavoured hand print.

"Yeah, I'm not sure that's gonna help," Sheni sighed, pinching the bridge of his nose. "Qualians might have low body temperatures, but I hardly think—"

The hand scanner whirred in confusion, glitched a bit, then turned a happy blue colour. The door to Mr. Zelewyn's office clicked open.

"You're a genius," Sheni said, beaming as he patted Alan on the head. "Now for the love of Jupiter, don't touch anything. With any luck, *I'll* be the one with sticky fingers..."

CHAPTER
FOURTEEN

The office belonging to Mr. Zelewyn was immaculate, refined, and surprisingly compact. The walls were lined with thin stalks of reed, though the plant didn't look native to the Queflian coastline; a rarer species shipped from further inland, perhaps, or even off-world. The carpet, like the one in the corridor outside, was plush and blue. For a few seconds, Sheni thought he'd stepped outside again, that Zelewyn's office – despite not being on the top floor – was open to the elements. There was no ceiling, only a perfectly azure sky blemished by only the thinnest strips of white, wispy cloud. Then he realised it was a projection – an incredibly lifelike one at that. Qualians were naturally outdoorsy. The manager of Nova Elysia could afford to maintain that illusion twenty-four seven. Even the cool, climate-controlled air tasted fresh and carried the faintest whiff of pine tree.

Sheni winced as a dollop fell from Alan's ice cream onto the floor. Gods, he hoped it was easy-clean.

"Stay there and don't fiddle with anything," he told his

little green accomplice. "With any luck we'll find the evidence we need and be on the phone to the Ministerium without Zelewyn ever knowing we were here."

Alan giggled and took a big chomp of cold, artificial mango.

Sheni began rummaging through the office's various wooden boxes and wicker baskets. Like many species in the galaxy, Qualians had long ago abandoned physical documents in favour of digital alternatives, but they were also rather traditional, and certain cultural rituals were still done the old way. Sheni hoped that extended to criminal activity managers wouldn't want the average extranet user to know about. He wasn't exactly a natural when it came to hacking people's data pads. And a fancy resort like this probably had top of the line cybernetic security, even on employees' portable devices.

But stealing stuff other people preferred to keep secret – *that* was something the crew of the *Silver Hart* knew a thing or two about.

Even so, he turned up nothing. He dug about on the shelves and in the strange hourglass-shaped cabinets at the rear of the room but had no greater luck there, either. Sheni sagged in defeat and listened to the sound of Alan slurping his ice cream. This wasn't going the way he hoped, and there was no backup plan. If they couldn't find something concrete with which to warn the Ministry, or the people of Porto Kumasa, then...

His eyes fell on Mr. Zelewyn's desk. He'd dismissed it at first, despite it being an obvious place to look, because it was so oddly shaped and narrow. And don't get him started on the chair. It was like an ice cream scoop, propped up at the angle of a medieval catapult in order to accommodate the

Qualians' question-mark shaped torsos. A holo-projector sat inert in the concave centre of the desktop. But now Sheni was behind it, he could see there *were* drawers set into its spindly sides. Or narrow alcoves, at least. He didn't know if they were supposed to be secret or not, but they were most certainly discreet.

Sheni crouched down and ran a finger over the groove around the hidden cavity. Gods, he hoped it wasn't locked. He had nothing to pick it with, and jamming it open with a knife or file was only a last resort. He had a suspicion this desk alone cost more than the rest of the room combined.

But when he pushed the narrow compartment gently inward, it popped open like the SIM card slot of an old smartphone.

Inside was a single data drive, a mere inch long and silver in colour.

"Result," Sheni said, beaming and holding up the data drive for Alan to see. Alan gurgled agreeably.

He plugged the data drive into the holo-projector. A high-resolution screen of documents beamed up from the table. Alan waddled over, one eye on the floating files and the other focused intently on what remained of his ice cream.

"Boring, boring, boring," Sheni muttered as he swiped through report after report. "Stars above, I hope these aren't just the freakin' accounts…"

He stopped, went back one slide. This wasn't a contract, or a spreadsheet, or an exhaustive receipt for fluffy dressing gowns and slippers. No, this was a set of blueprints, or perhaps a hypothetical design of some kind. Sheni had seen loads of schematics like this back when he used to scout out potential heist opportunities.

"Does this look like a map of the resort to you?" he asked

Alan. "Yeah, here's the Main Foyer with its big dome. And I guess this is where we are right now." He pointed further up the map. "The pools, the theatre... and here's the beach. Weird layout, though. The shoreline's not even halfway up the map. And the rest is..."

Ocean. The rest was the big, blue ocean. And yet it wasn't. The longer Sheni looked, the more anomalous structures jumped out at him – properties where no property ought to be...

"Hold on. There's no observation tower there in real life. Neither is there a massive two-storey revolving restaurant on the rocks over on the south side! And there definitely aren't any luxury condos floating in the middle of the freakin' sea..."

"Felonious displacement," Alan gurgled.

"This isn't just a map of Nova Elysia," Sheni said with a gasp. "This is a proposal for a massive resort expansion. *That's* why Mr. Zelewyn hired the poachers. He wants to drive out all the Plillup so he's free to build new facilities in their territory!"

This was it, he realised. This was surely all the evidence the Ministry would need to start an investigation. Sure, it didn't join all the dots, but it would hopefully get the ball rolling in time to stop Sylva's attack on Porto Kumasa.

Sheni was about to pull the data drive out and make the call when Mr. Zelewyn came sailing through the door.

"Mr. Dupont." Even now, surprised and clearly aware of Sheni's deception, Zelewyn's tone was polite and graceful. "What in the galaxy are you doing in my office?"

What in the galaxy. Wow. This guy was *pissed*.

"I was just, erm..." Sheni glanced at the hologram. "That is to say, you know, I was looking for the—"

Alan, who'd been standing by the desk only moments

earlier but was now somehow behind the door through which Zelewyn had entered, slammed it shut before jumping up and dumping what remained of his ice cream cone on the hotel manager's head.

Sheni wasn't sure what he was supposed to do afterward, so he raced forward and tackled Mr. Zelewyn around his oddly curved waist. Zelewyn threw his arms about, confused by the gelato dripping down his featureless face, and turned back to the door. Sheni struggled to hold the Qualian in position, and he doubted Alan's attempt to block the door would prove particularly effective, either.

Fortunately, it turned out Qualians weren't half as graceful when they were lugging a human-shaped weight behind them. Both Sheni and Mr. Zelewyn toppled to the floor where they flapped and wriggled about like a pair of trout on the deck of a fishing trawler. Alan grabbed Zelewyn's fleshy stump of a head with both of his sticky hands and somehow succeeded in dragging the hotel manager back toward the chair behind the desk, which Zelewyn collapsed into with flailing indignation.

"Stop this at once, gentlemen," Mr. Zelewyn snapped. "This is totally unacceptable behaviour. I have a mind to throw both of you off Nova Elysia grounds – with no refund!"

"Feel free to do that," Sheni replied, standing up and wiping his mouth with the back of his hand. "Inside the resort, outside – makes no difference. The Ministry's gonna find out about what you've done either way."

"What in the stars are you talking about?"

"Your expansion plans," Sheni said, nodding at the hologram.

"That's confidential material," Zelewyn said, turning their head-stump from the holo-projector to the hidden compartment in his desk. "How did you access this? It doesn't matter. These blueprints are nothing but hypothetical proposals. Every business does this. I hardly think the Ministerium will be any more concerned by these than they would a scribble on a napkin, Mr. Dupont."

"Yeah, maybe you're right. But I guess they might take these plans a bit more seriously once they know you're in league with Sylva and her band of poachers. We were at their camp, Mr. Zelewyn. We saw the explosives and heard you tell Sylva to blow up Porto Kumasa."

Mr Zelewyn went to protest his innocence, but Sheni raised his hand.

"Please, Mr. Zelewyn. Don't lie to us. You're much too polite for that."

Alan slammed his weedy fists against the tabletop and tried to look as intimidating as a smiling watermelon can.

"All right, very well." Zelewyn sighed back in his chair and tried to wipe the runny ice cream from his head. The cone remained stuck to him like a party hat. "You must understand, Mr. Dupont, it was never supposed to get this far. Those horrid poachers were supposed to have driven the Plillup from their homes more than a week ago."

"Oh, well that makes everything okay, then. Slaughtering their squid was a wonderfully humane way of getting them to vacate Porto Kumasa."

"Do you have any idea how valuable that territory is? Coastal bathing pools. Tours of the sunken ruins. *Underwater lodges*. But instead the authorities gifted it to a colony of outsiders. They shouldn't even be there!"

"But they *are* there. And they have been for hundreds of years, long before this resort. Whatever issues you have with Queflian immigration policies, you can't go around committing domestic terrorism just to make a few extra credits."

"You think I *want* to be evicting the Plillup? Please, Mr. Dupont. I'm the head concierge of the finest resort on Queflia. It's the shareholders who demand it. And if *I* can't deliver additional revenue opportunities, I assure you my replacement will!"

"You can't possibly tell me that Nova Elysia is underperforming," Sheni said, raising an eyebrow. "Even Gecki can't drink enough booze to make a dent in your profits."

"Of course it isn't. The resort is doing extremely well. But doing well isn't enough, not for our board of directors. In this business, if you're not continually growing, you may as well be going backward."

"That's utter nonsense." Sheni yanked the data drive from the holo-projector and pocketed it. "Why can't people ever be happy with what they have?"

"I dare say you wouldn't be able to afford a room here if you'd gone through life with *that* attitude, Mr. Dupont."

Sheni inhaled deeply through his nose.

"Alan, can you go fetch Xotl? I think we're gonna need a few extra hands."

Alan scurried out the door and reappeared ten minutes later with Xotl in tow. The plastic-wrapped Xocha was a little unsteady on their arms. They'd been at the coconut spritzes again.

"Oh, goodness," they spluttered. "Why does Mr. Zelewyn have an ice cream on his head?"

Sheni relayed everything to Xotl, discreetly passed them the data drive, then asked them to stand watch over the disgraced concierge until the Ministerium arrived. He'd already made the call while Alan had gone to collect the tipsy starfish. In the meantime, Alan tied the hotel manager to his chair with a length of stolen rope. Where Alan had stolen it from, Sheni didn't ask.

"Certainly," Xotl said, shaking their arms disappointedly at Mr. Zelewyn. "But what are *you* going to do?"

"Somebody's got to warn the Plillup," Sheni said, pausing in the office doorway. "Those poachers are gonna blow up Porto Kumasa whether we arrest this guy or not."

CHAPTER
FIFTEEN

Sheni marched out of the administration building via the same semi-concealed exit and followed the path through the dense ferns toward the shore. He was already at the dome that housed the majority of the resort's restaurants by the time Alan caught up with him.

"Are you sure you want to come with me, buddy?" Sheni asked, bending down with his hands on his knees. "Those Plillup weren't particularly pleased to see me the first time, you know."

Alan blew a bubble of spit from the corner of his mouth.

"Well, I guess they liked *you* well enough. Okay, then. But don't go running off, all right?"

Sheni took only a few more steps before he froze in his tracks. Something smelled damn good. His stomach growled in protest. That *kanelbulle* hadn't kept it quiet for long.

The circular doorway to a self-serve deli counter lay to his right. The lights inside were warm and cosy, the meats on the spits were glistening. And there wasn't a queue.

Well, he couldn't be expected to save a small civilisation on an empty stomach now, could he?

S heni stomped down the sands, hurriedly stuffing his mouth with handfuls of bread and meat. Alan tottered along beside him, chewing on a pterosaur drumstick.

"Five minutes," he muttered to himself in between guilty mouthfuls. "Five minutes won't make any difference, right?"

His first thought had been to hire another submersible. There was no way to get him and Alan down to Porto Kumasa without one. But then he remembered they'd never returned the first sub, that it was still lying broken on the beach of some deserted island, and something told Sheni that the old bug behind the counter wasn't likely to forget a face he'd seen only that very morning.

So instead they headed for the rocks jutting out on the northern side of the bay. Zelewyn's proposed expansion plans had featured an observation tower in that general vicinity, and the Garnidian attendant on the boat had told everyone not to approach the Plillup if they happened to see one there. Sheni was sure it had to be Porto Kumasa territory, or close enough to it that Zelewyn couldn't get planning permission. If he could find one of those Plillup, maybe he could relay word of the attack to Lord Bol'glossa. Whether the Plillup listened to him or not was down to them.

A short wooden railing had been erected in front of the rocks, warning guests that they were about to leave the resort. Sheni stepped over it, Alan scurried under it, and together they carefully navigated the damp, dark stones.

Much to Sheni's disappointment, he couldn't see any

Plillup – not in the water, not on the rocks, and not even amongst the jungle foliage further up. He decided to attract some attention.

"Look at me," he shouted, marching back and forth. "I'm a stupid human messing about where I shouldn't be."

Nothing, just the gentle crashing of waves and the cawing of gulls overhead. Sheni sighed and sat down on the rocks to pick at his food.

"I guess all we can do is wait."

Fifteen minutes later, two Plillup guards armed with pikes emerged from the sea, rising as the waves retreated. They didn't look best pleased to be paying Sheni a visit, and he wondered if they recognised him from the failed Mother Maw execution that morning. He slipped about on the rocks as he hastily climbed to his feet.

"I'm not here to cause any trouble," he said, holding out his hands to show them he meant no harm. They were shaking. "I'm here to help stop it. The poachers who've been attacking your squid – they're being paid to do it by the resort. But they won't stop there. They're going to plant bombs around Porto Kumasa and force you to flee your home. I just wanted to let you know. I can even show you where the poachers' camp is, if you want."

The two guards said nothing, only glanced sternly at one another. Then one of them reached behind their back and brought out a pair of organic-looking rebreathers Sheni recognised all too well.

"Come with us," the Plillup said, offering the masks.

"Oh, nah, that's all right." Sheni laughed nervously and took a step back up the rocks. "No offence, but I ain't going back down to your town, specially not when someone's trying to blow it up. I just came to warn you. But if you've got a map, I can—"

"Come with us," the other guard repeated, angling his pike toward Sheni.

"Okay, sure. Yeah." He held up his hands in surrender. "We'll go down to Porto Kumasa with you, won't we, Alan? Just don't feed us to that freakin' kraken of yours, you know?"

Sheni and Alan strapped the rebreathers to their faces – in Alan's case, the mask barely covered his grin, and his eyes swivelled freely to either side of it – and then waded into the water. An enormous squid lurked just beneath the waves where the seabed dropped suddenly, and harnessed to it with chains and kelp was an ornate bronze chariot carriage. Sheni and Alan struggled to swim out to it and had to be pulled into position by the impatient guards.

They held onto the carriage for dear life as the squid bunched its tentacles together, propelled itself with jets of water siphoned through its mantle, and plunged deep into the ocean's murky depths.

"Madam, haemoglobin red is *so* your colour."

Gecki bared her teeth in a grin. She was reclining on a stone slab in a humid *hammam* while a small Garnidian lady painted her claws and an insectoid Krettelian massaged oils into her dry scales. The Alpha Rhoden equivalent of Mongolian throat singing was being piped through the moist, arching walls.

This was the life.

Despite Gecki's best efforts to silence her mind and

enjoy the moment, she couldn't help wondering what the others were up to. Xotl was probably floating in a pool having passed out from their coconut allergy. Alan had likely eaten twice his own body weight and was now trying to dismantle the hotel's sprinkler system. And Sheni... well, Sheni was almost certainly sitting somewhere in the dark with his arms crossed, nursing a drink and feeling sorry for himself.

If they were smart, they were enjoying the resort's famous amenities as much as she was. Coz if the Ministry *did* catch up with Mr. Zelewyn following his deal with Sylva and her poachers, the doors to the Nova Elysia resort might not be open forever...

Next up, a quick bite to eat at the fishery. And maybe after that, a trip to the sim-rig cafe. According to the digital brochure on her room's menu screen, it even had a virtual hoverbike track complete with wind turbines and haptic feedback. Or perhaps she'd simply sprawl out on the beach with a drink or ten. She hadn't had a proper chance to bask in the sun all day.

Maybe she could even wrangle some of the others to join her.

Her Garnidian and Krettelian attendants finished their respective tasks, bowed politely, and then left Gecki alone to marinate a while. She liked it here in the *hammam*. The damp, echoey caverns reminded her of the temples back home. It was easy to forget a dance class for feathered cente-narians was taking place just on the other side of the wall.

She sighed and wriggled about on the slab. The thing was, deep down she knew Sheni *wasn't* off pining in a dim lounge on the opposite side of the resort. The dumb human was too stupid to do that. Moping about was a waste of time, sure, but it was mostly harmless. No, Sheni was too much of an idealist. Always had been, even when it came to planning heists. He couldn't push down his guilt and pretend to enjoy life like a normal person. He felt a compulsion to get involved, to fix problems that weren't anything to do with him... to be a *good person*, whatever the hell that was.

It was going to get him killed. There's a reason why most pirates are heartless bastards. The nice ones never last too long. And Sheni was a nice ex-pirate with a lot of money. Not exactly a recipe for survival, in or out of the business.

Gecki laid her head back against the stone and groaned. Sheni had gone back to Porto Kumasa to stop the poachers from blowing it up. She didn't know how she knew this to be true, but she knew it all the same. He wouldn't have the slightest clue how to prevent the bombing once he got there, but he'd find a way down there anyway.

She sat up and plucked the slices of star fruit from her eyes.

Godsdammit. The man was selfish, really, getting himself in these situations. Selflessly selfish.

But nobody else was gonna fish him out of it, were they?

CHAPTER
SIXTEEN

"... A nd that's why I had to make sure you were, you know, *aware*." Sheni put his hands on his hips and sighed. "Please don't kill me."

Lord Bol'glossa's attendants had been feeding him tiny fish when Sheni was escorted into his grand chamber. Now he had the leader of Porto Kumasa's full attention. About halfway through Sheni's explanation, he'd waved a webbed hand and half of the Plillup guards had sprinted off in search of outsiders planting bombs.

"You are not a poacher?" Lord Bol'glossa asked.

"No, I'm just a guest at the resort. I tried telling you before, but... Whatever. I didn't even know Porto Kumasa existed until after I checked in. We probably would have booked somewhere else if we'd known what Zelewyn was up to."

"Then you and your pet are friends of the Plillup. You must stay."

Alan giggled happily. Sheni grimaced and scratched the back of his neck.

"Ah, your excellence, thank you, but I really think I ought to—"

"You must stay," Bol'glossa repeated, "until this business with the poachers has been resolved."

"Of course." Sheni nodded in defeat. "It would be an honour."

Or it would have been this morning, Sheni added to himself. Before I knew the place was about to be blown up.

"Ensure our guests are fed and comfortable," Bol'glossa commanded, mirroring the way he'd treated Xotl and Alan that morning. "The rest of us must prepare for war."

"I just want to clarify," Sheni whispered to the guards who stepped forward to escort him out of the chamber. "I *am* the guest in that sentence, right, not the one being fed to them?"

He was halfway down the vine-painted glass tunnel when he froze and shot a look back toward the Plillup leader.

"Hold on, did Lord Bol'glossa say 'prepare for war'?"

"We cannot sit back and wait for the poachers to blow up our home or kill more of our squid," one of the guards replied, gently pushing Sheni forward. "This fight must be taken to them."

"Stars above. I only wanted to stop the violence, not point it in a new direction..."

The town square was an empty shell of its previously bustling self. The kelp-curtained shops, the hard coral pillars, the calligraphic bronze balconies and stone steps – everywhere was deserted. They hadn't even had time to pack away the trays of swamp cabbage and salted lionfish outside their doors. The locals must have retreated to more robust shelters carved into the surrounding rock, or perhaps even evacuated the town entirely. Sheni hoped he and Alan were being led to the same place as everyone else. Without a submersible, they were completely at the Plillup's mercy.

And if things turned bad, the poachers'.

Sheni watched as a small crab about the size of his shoe scuttled across the empty market and picked at the seaweed that congregated around the base of the pearl statue. It hurried into the shadows as Sheni and the guards crossed the plaza and passed through another lever-operated door on the opposite side.

The next corridor was similarly glass panelled, trimmed with nickel and decorated with swirling green flourishes, but with one minor difference: the floor was submerged under six inches of water. At first Sheni thought there'd been a leak, but the guards marched through the shallow pond as if nothing was out of the ordinary. Sometimes the Plillup just liked keeping their feet wet, Sheni guessed.

He squeezed the rebreather device in his hands. Thank the stars Alan was still wearing his. Who knew what bizarre infrastructure the Plillup had built down here. Sunken guest rooms? An elevator system comprised of alternating whirlpools? And how many atmospheres of pressure did the deepest neighbourhoods in Porto Kumasa reach? The Plillup might *look* frail in comparison to humans, what with their slender builds and squishy skin, but put them in the abyssal zone and it was a whole different story.

Gecki had been right about one thing, if nothing else. This wasn't his world. For all his good intentions, he didn't belong here.

The shadow of a great white whale thirty metres in length drifted over the top of their tunnel, clicking and cooing as its immense body cut out the lights of the neighbouring domes. Sheni stared slack-jawed. Alan waved like he was trying to attract the attention of a famous mudball player.

"Cetacean peduncle," he giggled through his mask, pointing to its tail.

"Quickly," one of the guards snapped, baffled as to what all the fuss was about.

Sheni grabbed Alan's hand and pulled him through the next door. Back to dry land, comparatively speaking. This part of Porto Kumasa appeared to be set into the neighbouring bedrock, though the entire right hand side of their present hall was an enormous portal like the one in the waterlock. The curved stone promenade was splattered with wet footprints and tiny pieces of seagrass, but the pit beneath the portal was deep like a scuba diving pool.

At its bottom, Sheni could just make out a pair of Plillup warriors suiting up for battle. But outside was where the rest of the forces gathered. A dozen or more flying squid with mantle armour. Plillup riders wielding flechette guns – rifles that fired needle-sharp darts, which travelled better through water than regular bullets. More of those giant lobster-monsters Sheni had seen the guards riding inside the domes, this time settled on the neighbouring coral caps. And at least thirty more Plillup warriors with pikes and bronze plate armour strapped around their tight-fitting shark-leather uniforms.

Not a bad sized battalion by any means. Enough to prevent anybody from planting bombs around the settlement, absolutely. But would it be enough to put a stop to the poachers for good?

Sheni wasn't so sure.

He and Alan were quickly ushered away from the portal, past another squad of Plillup rushing the other way, and through a small, round door into a plain room like the inside of a clay hut. There were no windows, no glass domes here. Just a lot of sponge-seats, a tray of sea cucumber and sushi slices, and a small rock pool in the room's centre. This was as far as they'd be going, he realised. When Sheni turned around again, only one of the guards remained in the doorway. The other must have stayed behind at the portal-pool.

"You will stay here," the guard said. "We will return when we need you."

"Okay, that's... Wait. What do you mean, when you need me? Need me for what?"

But the guard was already gone, locking the door as they went. Sheni threw up his hands as he reviewed their tiny quarters.

"Oh yeah, this is great," he mused. "Real secure, you know? I'd *much* rather have a million tonnes of rock fall on me than a tidal wave of water."

He sagged onto one of the admittedly soft chairs with a sigh. Alan had been eyeing the platter hungrily, and now he scooped the whole lot into his broad, dribbling mouth. Well, this was going to get dull quickly.

The door was unlocked not five minutes later.

"Woah, back already?" Sheni rose to his feet. "Is it time for... erm...?"

"No, it is not," the guard replied, exasperated. "You have a visitor."

The guard stepped to one side. To Sheni's immense surprise, it was Gecki who slinked grumpily through the squat door.

"Can't have you hoarding all the stupid for yourself," she rasped.

"How did you get down here, anyway?"

Sheni and Gecki sat on seats of sea sponge to either side of the rock pool while Alan fiddled with the seaweed creeping under the locked door. They hadn't heard any explosions during the time it took for Sheni to explain what he'd found in Mr. Zelewyn's office. That was probably a good sign.

"I figured you'd find a way to put yourself in the most dangerous position possible," Gecki rasped, "so I got us another submersible. I'm here to rescue you, ya big idiot."

"Are you seriously telling me that old bug leased us another sub? After what happened to the first one?"

"Well, he doesn't know about the first one yet, does he? And nah, course he didn't. I just sneaked round the back and borrowed one, didn't I?"

Sheni groaned and buried his head in his hands.

"At this rate, we'll be broke before we leave the resort..."

"Nah, don't be dumb. We'll use this new submersible to tow the broken one back to the hire shop. All that guy's customers are rich toffs. They probably break things all the time."

"Yeah, which obviously means the poor guy's gonna be super happy when we use a stolen sub to bring back a busted one..."

"At least we will be getting back," Gecki snapped. "If I hadn't nabbed that sub, you'd be stuck down here. Trapped in this room till you suffocated or drowned, probably."

"And now we both are."

"Yeah, there is that..."

An awkward silence fell between them. Alan filled it by stomping on the seaweed until its bladder sacs popped.

"Wait, what do you mean, rescue me?" Sheni suddenly

said. "I don't need rescuing! I mean, sure, I didn't exactly *want* to come down here, not while there's a freakin' battle going on, and yeah, I'm trapped in this room until the Plillup decide to let me out, but I'm not a *prisoner*. Not really. This is just for my wellbeing. I want to be here, kinda. I want to help, you know?"

Gecki raised her scaly equivalent of an eyebrow and stared at Sheni with her blind, milky eye until he averted his gaze.

"And giving the Plillup another person to worry about," she rasped. "That's helping, is it?"

"Being stuck down here isn't ideal, I'll admit that," Sheni replied, not looking up. "But I had to let them know the poachers were gonna bomb their town, didn't I? They'd have been totally in the dark otherwise."

"Yeah, I s'pose so." Gecki scratched her jaw. "Would have been a pretty miserable vacation, watching a bunch of degenerates blow chunks out of the water. Though I guess we'd have enough booze to hand to forget about it, wouldn't we?"

"Yeah. We had some grub in here, by the way. Looked pretty decent. Alan ate it."

"Course he did. Look, Sheni. I'm not trying to be hard on ya, you know? You've got a kind heart. Despite all the crap you've been through, cast out by your own people and all, you still want to do good. It's admirable. Or it would be, if it weren't gonna get you killed."

"I never wanted to be a pirate, you know? I mean, I'm grateful for everything you've done for me. I'd be dead if not for you. And we've had some great times over the years. But I've never been cut out for all the stealing and backstabbing. Or stabbing in general."

"Yeah, I know. This life ain't for everyone. Stars, it ain't even for *me* anymore, not since you found us that fancy sword and made us all rich. And you've made all of us better people, Sheni. This ain't a criticism. It ain't *bad* to be good, especially now we can afford to be. But you can't go running off to be the hero every time someone needs saving."

"Why not?"

"Coz you ain't a hero, Sheni. You're good, but that doesn't mean the same thing."

"I'm not a *superhero*, sure, but anyone can be a hero if they choose to do the right thing—"

"Nah. You're wrong. Running into a situation you've got no hope of surviving ain't heroic, Sheni. It's misguided. Foolhardy. Suicidal. It ain't enough to just *want* to do good. Not if you end up getting in the way – or making things worse."

"That's a pretty miserable way of looking at things, Gecki. And how have I made things worse? Porto Kumasa isn't getting blown up, thanks to me."

"Nah, it ain't," Gecki conceded. "Not yet, anyway. But you're acting like you're invincible, Sheni. Like everyone around you is rational and sensible and not gonna kill you for the fun of it. You know, like that Bol'glossa maniac tried doing this very morning. You're a lucky guy, but you ain't *that* lucky. One day you're gonna rush into something, get yourself killed, and have absolutely nothing to show for it. That ain't being a hero. That's being a fool."

"Yeah, maybe." Sheni bunched his shoulders and clasped his hands together in his lap. "But better a fool than a coward."

"I ain't a coward, Sheni. I just plan to live longer than you."

"But you sure can be heartless sometimes. So much for me making everyone in the crew a better person, huh?"

Gecki grumbled to herself.

"Look, I get what you're saying." Sheni sighed and turned to face Gecki. "Maybe I do have a habit of thinking of myself as a white knight, of taking on responsibilities that aren't, well, strictly my own. But we have to do *something*, you know? Because if we don't, who else will?"

"Bystander effect," Alan gurgled, happily splattering a polyp between his hands.

"The Ministerium," Gecki countered. "Or the local Queflian authorities. Or I dunno, somebody whose job involves flying around the galaxy saving those in need!"

"But the Plillup of Porto Kumasa can't rely on any of those people. Unfortunately, all they've got is us."

"You're not wrong there." Gecki bared her teeth in irritation. "And I'm not saying we should wash our claws of all responsibility, or whatever. But we ain't marines or mercenaries, and we don't have a freakin' nuclear-capable battlecruiser. We're just a bunch of ex-pirates who got lucky and scored big. There's gotta be a smarter, safer way we can do some good in this galaxy."

"Yeah, well." Sheni snorted and shook his head. "When you figure out what that is, let me know."

There was a *clunk* in the lock and the door swung open. Alan went rolling backward, seaweed still clutched in his tiny hands. The cantankerous guard from before lurked in the doorway.

"Hey, if it isn't our good friend Mr. Smiles," Sheni said, grinning nervously. "Is it over? Did you win?"

"Win?" The guard scowled at them as he tossed a bunch of armour on the floor. "No, topsiders. The battle hasn't even begun."

CHAPTER
SEVENTEEN

S heni struggled to get comfortable in the Plillup armour. For one, it was clearly made with a smaller physique in mind. Secondly, the bits it protected didn't necessarily correspond with the valuable assets of a human body. And thirdly, and this Sheni thought particularly important, he couldn't see how wearing a bunch of metal in the water was anything except monumentally stupid. Not unless they expected him to walk along the ocean floor as if he were inside a diving suit.

But he supposed it was better than heading into battle in just his Hawaiian shirt and swim trunks. And thank goodness he hadn't brought flip-flops.

"How does yours fit?" he asked Gecki, who was suiting up on the stone promenade beside him. All three of them already had their rebreathers on.

"They've given me the armour they put on their squid," she snarled. "My kind are hardly agile in the water at the best of times. How do they expect me to fight in this?"

"I don't think they do, really. I reckon they just don't want us to die."

"Then they should have left us in that stupid cave! Or let us take the submersible back to the surface!" Gecki gave up tying a sheath over her tail and tossed the metal aside. "Gah, I'd be a lot more use to these dumb fish people if they just let me stalk into the poacher camp in the dead of night. Hell, I could take half of them out in the daytime if they're in that much of a hurry."

"That wouldn't be very honourable, though. The Plillup see themselves as defending their home, not attacking the poachers."

"Pah. Semantics. It might not be honourable, but you get the same end result at a fraction of the cost. Ask those who are left widowed which they'd prefer."

The two guards from before watched them get ready with a blend of confusion and disdain. Alan was wearing a shin guard as a helmet and had somehow come into possession of a Plillup pike. Sheni gave up trying to attach a shoulder-plate and threw his hands up in defeat.

"I think this is as good as we're gonna get it," he said. "Where do you want us? Standing guard, here in the town? Or on the beach, covering their retreat?"

Both guards pointed into the portal pool next to them.

"In there."

"Yeah, that's what I was afraid you were gonna say," Sheni sighed, avoiding Gecki's choleric gaze.

Alan plopped into the pool and sank like a cannonball. Gecki and Sheni followed, lowering themselves slowly off the edge of the stone. They, too, sank to the bottom of the pool. Sheni found himself more capable of walking through the water with all his added armour than he expected, but there was still no chance of him swimming anywhere without taking everything off again. Gecki managed to wriggle a few feet off the ground before gravity took over.

Sheni approached the forcefield separating them from the wider ocean. It was a hell of a drop on the other side. Wherever the bottom was, light was having a much harder time reaching it than he would.

"I think we're gonna have a problem," he said to the guards swimming down through the pool beside him.

The two guards said nothing, just swam past him through the shimmering forcefield. Sheni turned to Gecki and shrugged. Maybe they wanted the crew to guard the portal instead. That was fine by Sheni. The second the Plillup were all gone, he'd strip off his armour, swim up to the surface and sprint back to Gecki's stolen submersible. He'd told the Plillup everything he knew about the poacher attack. Fighting for them had never been part of the arrangement.

But then the guards returned, carefully guiding a pair of enormous squid toward the portal. Neither squid was pulling a chariot-like carriage this time, Sheni noticed with a heavy feeling in his gut. They did have saddles wrapped around their mantles, though, which were kept from slipping off by their jagged fins. And a lot of armour plating on their tentacles, arms and underside. It was a small miracle they could still swim with all the added weight. Then again, Sheni reminded himself, this wasn't his world. Only the strongest were born from the abyss.

The squid retreated through the portal and into the waterlock pool, twitching their arms uncertainly. The guards stroked their webbed hands across the beasts' flanks to sooth them, then turned to the crew, their expressions hardening.

"Get on."

"Are you sure?" Sheni asked. "I mean, we're pretty heavy with all this armour, and I wouldn't want to—"

"There isn't time for your foolishness! Get on!"

Sheni approached the squid closest to him and gently laid a hand on its massive head. The creature's unblinking eye stared back at him. *What a strange fish*, it seemed to say. But for all the squid's nervousness regarding its retreat into the pool, it let Sheni climb onto its leather saddle without so much as a wriggle or a *bloop* or a skin-shimmer in discomfort. Opposite him, Gecki did the same (only with slightly less hesitation regarding the animal's wellbeing, her clawed feet dangling inches from the squid's exposed flesh). Seconds later, Sheni felt the unmistakeable weight of Alan on his shoulders, riding him like a backpack.

The two Plillup guards climbed on last, squeezing in front of Sheni and Gecki and taking the reins. The squid slowly returned to the wider waters, and Sheni's bowels liquified as they swam over a pit of pure blackness. Over to their right lay the caverns of Mother Maw, deeper still.

Unwilling to wrap his arms around the Plillup – and suspecting the Plillup would be even less keen – Sheni clutched the ridge at the rear of his saddle as tightly as he could as the squid made a rapid ascent toward the surface.

"You're not going to make it leap out of the water, are you?" he yelled at the Plillup in front of him. Sheni could speak through the water thanks to his rebreather mask, but he suspected their direction of travel meant the words weren't reaching his companion. "Hey, I said you're not going to—"

But the squid slowed down just before it broke the surface, where orange light sparkled and shifted like an oil fire. Perhaps he should have known, having watched them from the yacht; the squid sailed through the air backward, mantle first, their arms and tentacles trailing out behind them. The water spilled off him, and off the back of the great beast, and Sheni, instinctively gasping for air despite being perfectly capable of breathing while underwater, saw that there were dozens more squid all around them, each mounted by one or two Plillup warriors.

The rest of the day had passed him by, and the sky was now the colour of burnt amber, stricken by brushstrokes of dark purple and indigo. Far to their east stood the resort, a spattering of white and cream amongst an explosion of verdant green. To the west, a glittery horizon.

Besides the gentle lapping of the waves against the stoic forces of Porto Kumasa, all was quiet, and all was still.

"What do these maniacs expect me to do from the back of a squid?" Gecki rasped from the cephalopod next to him. "They didn't even give us weapons."

"I don't see any poachers, so maybe we won't need any. Do you think maybe they caught wind of the Plillup defences and got scared away?"

Gecki squinted down the coastline with her one good eye.

"Nah, they ain't scared. They're just making sure they hit this place with everything they've got."

Sheni shielded his eyes from the setting sun and followed Gecki's gaze. Just visible against the coastline were three large skiffs, skipping above the waves toward them on their quaking thrusters, churning the water into steam.

The Plillup riders opened the kelp satchels attached to the front of their saddles and passed flechette rifles back to Sheni and Gecki. Sheni took his reluctantly.

"I get us near," the Plillup warrior in front of Sheni said, "and you shoot."

Sheni stared at the gun in his hands. It fired needle-like projectiles instead of bullets so that it worked just as well underwater as it did in the open air, and all sorts of buttons and latches were built into its engraved nickel casing, but he understood the general principle.

"Yeah, you bet I will," he replied, swallowing hard.

D eep in her ink-black cavern, Mother Maw stirred restlessly.

Something was wrong. She could sense it in the electrical signals emitted by her shoal, her brood. Danger. Death. The waters reeked of it.

She surged back and forth between her caves, crashing into the subaquatic bulwarks, wrestling amongst a forest of reeds. No way out. Trapped. Safe, for now. But not forever. A mother without her children – no mother at all.

The queen of the squid drew her colossal beak to the cave mouth and squeezed her arms and tentacles out into the wider pit, up toward the stone steps and the twinkling lights of Porto Kumasa. Each monstrous probing limb found a basalt mound or a pillar of coral, and pulled.

Stone split and rocks crumbled.

Cracks began to show.

CHAPTER
EIGHTEEN

When the poacher ships came within five hundred metres of Porto Kumasa, the Plillup attacked.

With a warbling battle cry from its rider, Sheni's squid surged forward on its jets. Sheni held on for dear life as they careened through the suddenly choppy water. Alan clutched at his neck and dangled out behind like a badly ironed cape. A strap of ultra-strong kelp was all that kept the rifle from flying out of his white-knuckled hands.

"I can't... see... what's happening!" he yelled as they dipped in and out of the water.

They plunged deep with no warning, and all around him Sheni saw other squid doing the same. There were too many bubbles and blurs to see clearly – for a *human* to see clearly, at any rate – but Sheni thought he spotted a white maelstrom a short distance ahead.

What temperatures could the Plillup withstand, he wondered? They powered their town using geothermal vents, after all. He hoped they didn't pilot the squid through the wakes left by the poachers' skiffs. He'd slow-cook like a jacket potato, especially wrapped in all this stupid metal armour.

But then they were on the rise again, the whole shoal as one, and the next thing Sheni knew their squids were clear of the water, flying forward – not backward as he'd seen from the yacht – with their arms and tentacles bunched tight together like a bronze-tipped bouquet. The first of the three skiffs was right beside them, its upper deck teeming with poachers rushing to man the ship's harpoons. And then the limbs of Sheni's squid opened like a fleshy flower blooming in fast-forward, and out the tentacles whipped, slashing some poachers across the chest and grabbing others before dragging them back down into the drink.

It happened so quickly, Sheni didn't even think to shoot anyone.

He watched as his squid, one tentacle wrapped around the midriff of the poacher it had pulled underwater, speared its victim through the torso with a metal-plated arm and left the corpse to spew out a cloud of blood behind them. Then it was headed upward again, and this time Sheni took one hand off the saddle in order to raise his rifle roughly in the right direction.

No sooner had they broken the surface than a harpoon plunged into the water beside them. Sheni panicked and pulled his trigger, but the flechettes from his rifle only peppered the side of the skiff. That would teach him for trying to shoot one-handed.

The shot at them had missed, but other Plillup riders weren't so lucky. A dozen metres to Sheni's right, a second hooked spear impaled a squid through its olfactory crest, just below its mantle, and a Plillup floated face down in the waves further ahead, his slender, turquoise back peppered with bullet holes. Sheni looked around in a panic, but his search for Gecki was cut short as his aquatic steed once again dove deep underwater.

He'd hoped it would at least be quiet beneath the waves, but it was somehow even worse. The sound carried. Every boom of a harpoon became a roll of thunder, every whizz of bullets cutting through the water a serpent's hiss. Sheni wanted to shut his eyes and drown it out, to magically will himself back to the isolated tranquility of the resort. He didn't want to fire his gun again. It wasn't just that he didn't like firearms all that much – he didn't even know how many flechettes he had left, or what he was expected to do when it came time to reload.

Stars above, he really ought to listen to Gecki in future.

The Plillup guard riding Sheni's squid directed it to swim right under the skiff presently taking shots at them. Sheni ducked even though the squid left him plenty of headroom. He was just thinking how lucky he was that these ships ran on thrusters, not propellers, when he spotted another squid wriggling through the turbulent waters not far from them. Gecki was riding on its back, her teeth bared in a furious snarl behind the visor of her mask.

Sheni would have sighed with relief if the constant pressure on his chest hadn't been so immense. All three of them were still alive. So far.

"You're gonna have to disable those harpoon cannons," he shouted to the Plillup in front. "You'll never win this fight if you don't. They'll keep picking you off, one by one."

"We will triumph," the guard snapped back.

"There are more dead Plillup in the water than poachers, friend."

The rider appeared to consider this for a moment, then whistled to their comrade – a short, high-pitch tweet that travelled rapidly through the water like a dolphin click.

Their two squids drew close. Sheni gave Gecki a thumbs-up, and in return she shook her head menacingly. He knew what that look meant – if somehow they survived this mess, she'd kill him. Then his rider made a series of quick hand movements, the other Plillup nodded, and their two squid rapidly headed back to the surface.

Back to the side of the skiff.

"Erm, what are we doing?" Sheni asked.

"You will disable the harpoons," the Plillup yelled back.

"What do you mean, I will?" They broke the water. "You're the warrior here, not me!"

The Plillup turned in the saddle and, with a furious and desperate expression on his pale-scaled, black-eyed face, shoved Sheni's rifle back into his arms.

"You have protected a ship before, yes?"

"Well, yeah, the yacht I guess, but—"

"Then protect *this* ship from the poachers, too! Go!"

Sheni hesitated, but Alan was already halfway up the rungs embedded in the side of the skiff. He knew the Plillup rider and his squid would be killed if they lingered this close to the poachers for much longer, so he swung his rifle onto his back and climbed onto the ladder. A second later, his ride was gone.

"Hold up, Alan," he hissed. "You don't even have a gun!"

The little green lunatic disappeared onto the upper deck. Sheni shot a panicked glance down the flank of the ship's hull, but it didn't seem as if any of the poachers on board had noticed either of them making the climb.

He poked his head up over the edge of the skiff. Mostly he just saw boots rushing this way and that. Alan, of course, was nowhere to be seen. But he wasn't totally alone. Directly opposite him, hanging onto the rungs on the other side of the ship, was a familiar, scaly green face.

Gecki nodded down the deck as if to say, *Go on, then.* Sheni shook his head, frozen in fear. Gecki rolled her eye, tried changing the colour of her scales to match the ship before remembering she was half-covered in metal plates and a rebreather mask, and then lurched onto the deck with a low, guttural growl. Sheni gritted his teeth and pulled himself up after her.

He immediately came face to face with the poacher manning the bow-facing harpoon cannon. Sheni pulled the trigger of his rifle without thinking and rattled off a burst of needles. The poacher dropped to the deck, moaning and clutching at the holes in his stomach.

"I'm sorry," Sheni said, grimacing. "Well, not really, but sort of, you know? Stars above, I don't like this…"

He took cover behind a steel crate overlooking the rest of the upper deck. Flying squid soared through the air to either side of the ship, their riders firing upon the other two skiffs with flechette rifles of their own. Sheni watched as one rider threw her pike right through an insectoid poacher, who stumbled backward, their mouth opening and closing like a speared guppy, before tumbling into the turbulent waters on the other side of the ship.

Gecki was already halfway across the deck, forgoing her rifle to instead slash at the poachers with her claws. Blood splashed across the wooden boards and the steam from spilled intestines blended with the mist and drizzle conjured by the skiff's rickety, spluttering thruster. Which, Sheni noticed, was presently being battered by Alan. The tiny guy was standing on top of it, hopping from foot to foot as if walking on hot sand again, whacking the engine with a stolen harpoon.

The idiot would get them all blown up.

One of the poachers turned toward Gecki with a plasma

rifle in their hands. Sheni shot up from behind his metal box and sprayed them with flechettes. They were dead before their body hit the deck. Another poacher came running down to take their place. Pretty soon they were dead, too.

Sheni had an unpleasant suspicion that he actually wasn't too bad at this, and he didn't like that idea one bit.

Still, he kept his finger on the trigger, defending Gecki from anyone who might try and stop her from mauling every poacher in sight... until the rifle projected nothing but a series of dry clicks.

He checked the gun for a second clip, but the rifle was dead. And he would be too, if he didn't get the hell off this ship.

Sheni felt the tip of a snub-nose revolver dig into the small of his back, and went rigid.

"Toss that rifle over the side," Sylva said. "I know it's empty, but I ain't taking no chances."

Sheni did as he was told. The rifle plopped into the water; Sheni expected it to sink, but it just bobbed there. At the same time, he watched as two poachers smacked Gecki around the jaw with their rifles and stood over her, ready to shoot, as she lay sprawled and dazed on the floor.

"Honestly, I barely even care what's happening here anymore." Sheni raised his hands above his head and sighed. "I just want to go back to the resort. Nah, scratch that. I just wanna go home."

"I don't know how you troublemakers got out of the cage back at camp," Sylva said behind him, "but you ain't never getting out of this one, I promise you that."

Sheni winced as Sylva jabbed the revolver into his back, expecting to hear an explosion – presuming he lived long enough after the shot to hear anything at all. He glanced back at Sylva as he stumbled toward the steps leading down to Gecki. Her face was a tempest of delirious fury. He couldn't see any door through which she could have ambushed him. She must have climbed up from a hatch in the floor, or perhaps even scaled the outside of the skiff.

Gecki nodded to Sheni as he was shoved onto his knees beside her, then tore off her mask. Sheni did the same. If they were going to die here, they'd at least do it breathing fresh air.

Cragg, the poacher who'd put them in Sylva's cage that morning, marched toward Sheni and Gecki from the opposite end of the ship, holding Alan upside-down in front of him by one of his spindly legs. He dumped Alan onto the deck before quickly stepping out of retaliatory range.

"Ex-pirates living the high life," Sylva snarled. She waved her revolver at them wildly. "You could have gone anywhere, done anything in the galaxy you wanted. So why in the stars would you team up with this bunch of seaweed-wearing losers?"

"Coz we don't like bullies," Sheni replied. "And we *especially* don't like bullies who profit from other people's misery."

"Ah, so you're hypocrites. Gotcha. Good to know what you are, coz you spineless fools sure ain't pirates no more, probably never were, and only the gods know how you ever scored so big..."

Sheni tuned out. Something monstrous had blotted out the setting sun and cast a shadow over the skiff. A few of the poachers saw it, too, and were rushing to grab the biggest weapons to hand.

"...and to think what you could have achieved, working on a crew like mine." Sylva bent down and glared at them.

"What are you idiots gawping at? Have I got something stuck in my teeth?"

"Nah," Sheni replied, his face numb as he stared past her shoulder. "But I have a feeling *someone* will pretty soon..."

A dark purple tentacle the length of the *Silver Hart* had extended out from the sea behind Sylva and was probing the warm evening air. Another had coiled itself around the skiff's thruster as if trying to choke the life out of it. The longer they all stared, the more pink and suckered appendages snaked up from around the three ships. The ocean churned. And all the while, their skiff rose further and further out of the water.

The kraken tightened her grip. The deck began to crack. Sylva lowered her revolver and backed away, her bony, ridged face suddenly drained of all colour.

"Everybody," she screamed. "Abandon sh—"

"Nah, you're staying." Gecki grabbed Sylva by the throat, cutting her off mid-word. "A good captain always goes down with her ship, right?"

Sylva's crewmates were far too focused on saving their own skin to care what happened to their boss. Gecki threw Sylva across the deck and into the base of the belching, shuddering thruster, where she sat groaning and listing from side to side.

"Seriously, though," Gecki rasped to Sheni and Alan. "We'd better leave."

Together they sprinted to the side of the skiff and leaped. They hit the water with a sharp, cold splash that knocked the wind from Sheni's lungs. He panicked and flailed about. If only he hadn't taken off his rebreather mask. And now he was sinking, dragged toward the abyss by the weight of his stupid armour. Squinting painfully through the saltwater, he saw the colossal head of Mother Maw. Its silhouette stretched down far below his feet. Eels and manta rays raced past him in the opposite direction. The question Sheni asked himself wasn't whether he was destined to become fish food, only whether or not he'd drown before they started nibbling.

Then somebody grabbed the collar of his Hawaiian shirt and Sheni felt himself rise toward the surface.

Warm air enveloped his face and he gasped for breath. Looking over his shoulder, he recognised his saviour as the Plillup rider he'd gone into battle with. They both smiled with hysterical relief. Clambering onto the squid's saddle once more, Sheni was glad to see that Gecki and Alan had also been rescued. Both were standing unsteadily on the mantle of the other guard's squid, watching Mother Maw lift Sylva's ship almost twenty metres off the surface of the sea.

A figure, barely visible against the bruised sky, stumbled to the edge of the raised skiff. Sheni heard Gecki hiss with frustration. So much for going down with the ship when the ship insisted on rising up instead. Sylva was going to escape.

But then, an instant before Sylva could jump to safety, one of the kraken's tentacles cracked the skiff in half. Sylva tumbled backward into its exposed cargo hold. And the gigantic finned head of Mother Maw burst from the sea, a thousand tonnes of eldritch flesh, and it closed its enormous hooked beak around the skiff with an asteroid-cracking *crunch*. Wood and metal splintered out like grenade shrapnel. The resulting wave from Mother Maw's re-entry into the sea almost knocked Sheni off his squid again, and probably caused a small tsunami back at Nova Elysia. The few poachers still manning the remaining two skiffs jumped overboard before the same thing could happen to them.

"Gotta love a matriarchal society," Gecki rasped, grinning as the kraken's tentacles continued to wreak havoc on the intruders. "You know, this would have gone a lot quicker if you Plillup had let her out from the start."

The remaining Plillup riders skimmed through the choppy waves, picking off stragglers. A few poachers had gotten away and were swimming desperately for the distant shore. Sheni collapsed onto the mantle of his squid and hacked up a lungful of seawater.

"I don't know about you, Gecki," he shouted, "but authentic or not, I could really do with an all-inclusive bar right about now."

CHAPTER
NINETEEN

S heni, desperate for a drink of anything that didn't have copious amounts of salt in it, asked to be taken back to the shoreline. But the Plillup had other plans. He and Gecki were handed spare rebreathers and forced to ride the squid back down to Porto Kumasa.

Mother Maw continued to ravage the skiffs for a while, plucking the occasional unfortunate poacher from the water and flinging them miles into the sunset, but finally chose to return to her caverns, the entrance to which was now cracked wide open. Much of the carved stonework around the edge of the pit was destroyed. Sheni watched as the immense beast sank past them to the ocean depths like the Titanic, flanked by dozens of giant squid and schools of returning fish.

"Where are you taking us?" Sheni asked the guard.

"To speak with Lord Bol'glossa," the guard replied, and then he turned back to tug on the reins as if that was all that needed to be said on the matter.

"I need to get that submersible I borrowed, anyway," Gecki said from the next squid over.

"You presume we're ever leaving again," Sheni mumbled to himself.

His guard said nothing.

Their squid performed the same manoeuvre as before, reversing through the forcefield portal into the waterlock pool for Sheni, Gecki and Alan to disembark. Sheni and Gecki stripped out of their armour and swam up to the surface. Alan refused to take his makeshift helmet off and had to be carried up by the two guards, who seemed not to dislike Alan quite as much as they did the others.

"Gods," Gecki snarled as she collapsed onto the stone promenade beside the pool. "It's good to be on solid ground again."

"Get up," one of the guards snapped, plopping Alan down beside her with a clang. "Lord Bol'glossa is waiting."

"Come on, Gecki." Sheni shrugged. "Let's get this over and done with, yeah?"

They were escorted back through the city, and Sheni was at least relieved to see that the market square was slowly returning to its usual self. Plillup filed back into the busy dome, tidying up the stalls they'd left behind in a panic and shooing the curious crabs that had come to pilfer shrimps while they'd been away. A small gaggle of Plillup children sprinted through the maze of coral, the slapping of their webbed feet almost as loud as their laughter, excited to be back home.

"Whatever happens," Sheni said to Gecki as they followed the ornate tunnel to Bol'Glossa's chamber, "it's nice to know we did some good, right?"

Gecki replied with a bitter growl.

The three of them were brought before Bol'Glossa, who remained sat in his delicate throne of golden curls, a pair of giant lobsters standing watch on the other side of his chamber's panoramic window. Sheni half expected to have his legs kicked out and be forced to kneel, but it was instead Bol'Glossa who rose to greet them.

"Outsiders," he warbled. "Now you are friends."

Lord Bol'Glossa laid a massive webbed hand on each of their heads and pressed down firmly. Sheni tried not to breathe. The Plillup leader smelled of cod and eggy sulphur. When Bol'Glossa removed his hands, both their heads were covered in a thin film of slime.

"Well, that was nice," Sheni whispered to Gecki, who looked about ready to disembowel him.

"Bestow upon them Shawls of Courage," Lord Bol'glossa demanded.

"The shawls of what, now?"

Short cloaks of kelp decorated with pearls and beads of opal were suddenly plunged over their heads. Gecki hissed in surprise. Sheni's green shawl seeped fresh seawater into his shirt and made a puddle around his boots. Its odour was very... *salty*.

"Thank you, your excellency," Sheni said. "You're much too—"

"And for your brave pet," Bol'Glossa continued, "the tastiest fish from our freshest catch."

Much *ooo*-ing and *ahh*-ing spread around the chamber as the frightened Plillup they first saw upon entering the settlement that morning approached holding a huge salmon-ish creature, five foot long and covered in weird, wormy lumps. It was offered to Alan lengthways like a ceremonial sword. Alan took it excitedly in his weedy arms, tried and failed to fit the whole thing in his mouth, and then cuddled it and gurgled with delight.

"You've been much too kind," Sheni finished, bowing respectfully.

"And yet I must ask you to leave. We Plillup need to process today's events, and we must do so together as a people, alone. But you are now friends of the Plillup. You are welcome back in Porto Kumasa at any time."

Sheni, Gecki and Alan bowed as Lord Bol'glossa returned to his throne, then were escorted back to the Elkhorn waterlock by a procession of guards. They were already halfway through the market before Sheni leaned over Gecki and whispered, "So we're never coming back here again, right?"

"Not while I still have scales on my body," Gecki snarled, hurrying her pace.

They splashed down the steps of the waterlock and waded toward Gecki's borrowed submersible. It was only a two-seater, Sheni noticed. Alan might be small, but it would still be a squeeze.

"Leave the fish, Alan," Gecki rasped. "I don't want it stinking up the sub."

Alan hugged the dead salmon as if it were a giant teddy bear he'd won at the fairground.

"What do you want that fish for, anyway?" Gecki asked. "They'll have tastier fish back at the resort, believe me."

Alan slapped the fish against the side of the sub.

"Gods, fine. Just keep it away from me, all right?"

They squeezed inside, Sheni and Gecki sitting in the small, cramped seats up front with Alan and his smelly fish crammed into the storage cubby behind. Gecki switched on the jets and slowly reversed the sub out of the portal. The assorted Plillup guards stood at the top of the steps and watched them leave.

"Please get us back to the resort so I can take off this horrible shawl," Sheni said through a fake smile as he waved goodbye.

"Absolutely," Gecki rasped. "But first, we need to find that deserted island..."

The old bug in the hire shop tottered out from behind his counter. There'd been all that palaver over in the bay not one hour ago, and now there was a lot of banging and clanging coming from inside his workshop. He couldn't help worrying one of those awful poachers had gotten in.

He pushed aside the partition wall and crept through, socket wrench at the ready.

No poachers, and no Plillup. Maybe it was just a juvenile pterosaur, he wondered. They got confused sometimes, mistaking the shiny tools for the shimmering scales of fish, and struggled to fly back out again. But although a can of ultramarine blue paint had been knocked over, and a lot of pearly seaweed had been dumped on the floor, the workshop was deserted. He lowered the wrench and put his bristly clawed hands on his thorax instead.

"Well I never. Where in the galaxy did *you* come from?"

Two of his submersibles bobbed gently at the bottom of his boat ramp. They were tethered together with some kind of industrial-strength kelp. One was the sub he'd loaned out to that dodgy group of weirdos that morning. Its engine was busted, that much was obvious, but the chassis itself still looked watertight. He hadn't even realised the other sub was missing.

"Gonna be a lot of paperwork for this," he muttered to himself, glancing up in the direction of the resort. "But I think the boss has bigger fish to fry..."

S heni, Gecki and Alan stomped up the beach toward the hotel complex. Alan dragged his massive salmon behind him. It was now so coated with sand that it looked battered and deep fried.

They hadn't even reached the sun loungers when they heard the first of the resort's guests speaking in hushed, worried voices. Clearly something big had happened at Nova Elysia while they were away. Sheni and Gecki shared a glance, then hurried their pace, first to a jog, then an all-out sprint through the fern-flanked outdoor paths.

If anything had happened to Xotl...

The commotion led them all the way through the resort to the Main Foyer. The receptionists were standing on the wrong side of their desk looking confused and distraught. An Oortilian member of staff was crying. Sheni assumed the Qualian employees were just as upset, perhaps even more so, but they were so unflappable it was sometimes hard to tell.

Mr. Zelewyn was being escorted out through the front archway of Nova Elysia by a pair of burly Ministerium executors. His hands were mag-cuffed. A black armoured cruiser, its wings pulled back like a dragonfly's, waited for him in the lantern-lit courtyard outside.

"Have you seen Xotl?" Sheni asked one of the shell-shocked receptionists. "They're starfish shaped, purple, about this tall. Hello? Are you listening to me?"

"I'm quite all right," Xotl said, cartwheeling into the conversation. Sheni relaxed. "I would have been rather bored, in fact, had I not been so worried about you and Alan. I heard about the big battle."

"What about me?" Gecki snarled.

"I didn't even know you'd gone," Xotl replied matter-of-factly. "I assumed you were still in the spa."

"I *did* think your claws were looking nice," Sheni added.

"Yeah, well," Gecki said dismissively. "Gonna have to get them done all over again, ain't I?"

"The Ministry took my call seriously, then," Sheni said. "Gonna be honest. I kind of thought they'd ignore me."

"Well, the two officers they sent certainly didn't consider your accusations particularly credible at first," Xotl replied. "Even when I showed them the blueprints you found, they appeared more concerned that we'd tied Mr. Zelewyn up than by any hypothetical construction he might have planned. But then poachers started to wash up on the beach, screaming about a kraken and threatening to kill Zelewyn for not telling them how dangerous the bomb job was, that the Plillup were supposed to be stupid, defenceless fish people. They put the cuffs on him pretty quickly after that."

"And the surviving poachers, too, yeah?"

"No, Sheni. They booked the poachers into the honeymoon suite, free of charge. Of *course* they arrested the poachers."

"So, that's everything, right?" He gave the crew a hopeful look. "The Plillup of Porto Kumasa are safe. Both the submersibles are back at the hire shop. Mr. Zelewyn and the poachers are either dead or behind bars. Alan has a fish. I think it's all over, you know? I mean, I know *my* conscience is clear."

"Finally," Gecki rasped, "we can do what we freakin' *came* here to do. Eat. Drink. *Relax*."

"Ah, yes. About that." The plastic of Xotl's enviro-suit squeaked as their arms wilted. "You might find relaxing harder than you think..."

CHAPTER
TWENTY

The crew of the *Silver Hart* sat under the leafy roof of the beach-side bar, listening to the moonlit waves lapping against the shore. Sheni felt exhausted, his eyes and legs leaden in equal measure. It had been one hell of a day.

They had the beach almost entirely to themselves, though the Mansa couple Sheni had seen pottering around the resort were sitting in the sand about forty metres further down the beach. Everybody else was either loitering around the various concourses in states of shock or had already packed up, trekked through the jungle to their ships and left.

The Ministry officers hadn't just arrested Mr. Zelewyn. They'd shut down the whole resort. Nova Elysia was off-limits to the public, pending further investigation.

"No good deed goes unpunished," Sheni mumbled to himself.

"What was that?" Xotl asked.

"Oh, nothing. Just that this hardly feels like a reward for

saving the Plillup, you know? It would have been nice if they'd kept the massage parlour open, at least."

"Eh, if you want everything to stay as it is," Gecki rasped, "sometimes you've gotta stick your head in the sand. We'll probably get a refund, though, so that ain't too bad."

Sheni leaned across the counter and picked at the basket of churros they'd pilfered from an abandoned food stall. A silvery figure gleamed in the moonlight. It was the automata bartender from inside, come to collect his tips.

"Hey, man," Sheni yelled, waving. "Any chance we can get some drinks over here?"

"Not on your life, fleshy," the automata replied in monotone. "I don't work here anymore. Pour your own drinks."

Sheni and Gecki turned to each other and shrugged.

"Don't mind if I do," Gecki rasped, climbing over the counter.

Under the soft orange glow of oil lanterns, the reptile rummaged through the various liquor bottles and bamboo cabinets and refrigerators. Eventually she emerged holding two mugs.

"Thought I'd keep it simple," Gecki said, handing a beer to Sheni. "Don't know where they keep the little umbrellas, anyway."

"Nobody else knows how to make those coconut spritzes," Xotl spluttered mournfully. "There goes *that* vice."

"It's probably for the best, Xotl," Sheni replied, giving the starfish a sympathetic pat on the arm. "Allergies are no joke. A few more of those cocktails and you'd have blown up inside your enviro-suit like a balloon."

"I suppose there's not much use in a getaway pilot who's always intoxicated, anyway."

"I dunno, most pirate crews manage it," Gecki said.

They drank their beers thoughtfully and watched the stars reflect on the gentle water. Gecki had brought out a pitcher of kwagua juice, too, but Alan wasn't interested. He was too busy waddling back and forth along the beach instead. Making the most of his remaining time on Queflia, Sheni supposed.

"I guess tonight's our last night, then," he said with a sigh. "What do we do now? Like, where do we even go?"

"Could head to the Corpse & Casket, I suppose," Gecki rasped.

"I dare say we can afford to visit somewhere a little less repugnant," Xotl replied. "Somewhere on Kapamentis, perhaps. Or we could just find another resort. There are plenty of alternatives here on Queflia, even."

"Yeah, but then what?" Sheni sipped his beer. "We can't just hop from one resort or dive bar to the next. What's the *plan*, you know?"

"Plans." Gecki scoffed. "Like we've ever had a plan, Sheni."

"Yeah, we have. They've usually been simple – steal this, break into that, try not to get shot – but there's *always* been a plan in place. Or at least a goal. Something to do, something to aim for. Drinking ourselves into a stupor... I dunno, it just feels like we're drifting. Can't do this forever."

"What are you saying? You want to pull another job, or something?"

"No, of course not. We all agree we're not pirates anymore, right? You know, like it was just a way for us to make enough credits to get out of that game for good."

Xotl bent their arms in agreement. Gecki bobbed her scaly head from side to side.

"Yeah," she said reluctantly, "that and make a name for myself. But we found the legendary Sword of Bokata, so now *we're* legends too. Ain't no point in risking our necks for credits when we've already got more credits than we can spend, right?"

"Exactly. So no more thieving, not unless it's for the right reasons. Whatever those might be."

"Sheni, hold on a minute, will ya?" Gecki squinted at Sheni with her piercing yellow eye. "Surely you ain't suggesting we fly around the galaxy saving those in need. Have you learned nothing from today?"

"I learned that we can do a lot of good by *being* good," Sheni replied.

"You can do a lot of stupid by being stupid, too. I told you, we ain't heroes. It just ain't in our blood, you know? Can you honestly tell me you *enjoyed* what we went through today? That you felt even the tiniest bit in control?"

Sheni took a deep breath and considered this.

"Nah, it was pretty horrible," he conceded. "I've never felt more out of my depth than when riding into battle on the back of a giant squid. All I wanted to do was run back to the resort, or the ship, or anywhere else in the freakin' galaxy. But can *you* say you didn't feel even a little good, standing up for those who needed us?"

"Course I did," Gecki rasped, picking a bit of churro out of her teeth. "I'm not saying we should turn a blind eye" – she peered at Sheni with her milky pupil – "to all the bad stuff in the galaxy. But we ain't cut out for that merc life, and you know it. We've gotta stop looking for trouble, Sheni. Let the trouble come to us, if it has to. We attract enough of it as it is."

"If we wanted to play dice with our lives," Xotl added kindly, "we could have stayed being pirates. At least that way we'd get paid sometimes."

"Yeah, I guess so." Sheni shrugged. "But there's gotta be *something* productive we could be doing with our time, you know?"

"Something that plays to our strengths and experiences," Xotl suggested.

"What, like stealing things?" Gecki snorted. "Good luck with that."

Sheni took a long swig of beer and watched Alan playing in the sand. Wreckage from the poacher skiffs was still washing up onto the beach. A splintered plank here, a rusted bolt there. The occasional leg. The little guy was scurrying between pieces of flotsam, dropping one in favour of another, the way a child might collect seashells.

"Sometimes," he said, "I think we'd all be happier if we were more like Alan. Look how content he is. Just minding his own business, collecting junk like it's actually worth something."

"Hey," Gecki rasped. "One person's junk is another's treasure, right?"

After a moment of silence, all three turned to face one another.

"It is my understanding," Xotl suggested coyly, "that private and commercial ships go missing far more often than people think. Somebody has to find out what happened to them."

"Some of them even crash," Sheni added. "Which means someone's gotta sort through the wreckage to retrieve any valuable cargo, too. You know, before the vultures arrive and pick it clean."

"A job like that's probably in high demand," Gecki mused, "what with corpo-clients not wanting to get their hands dirty and accept culpability, that kinda thing. I bet it pays good."

"Of course, only a crew with a healthy wallet could afford to invest in that kind of business," Sheni pointed out. "You'd need the right ships, the right crew. You've gotta spend credits to make credits, right?"

"Absolutely. But spacers with a tonne of money, the time to focus on a new enterprise *and* who have specialties in identifying and recovering lost valuables? They're gonna be hard to find."

"Hmm. Yeah." Sheni crossed his arms. "Shame."

Sheni and Gecki caught each other's eye, then broke into mischievous laughter. Xotl flexed their five arms and dilated their suckers in amusement.

"To the Silver Hart Salvage Company," Gecki said, raising her mug in a toast.

"I was gonna suggest Sheni's Salvage," Sheni replied with a wink, "but I suppose your name will do just fine."

Xotl wrapped an arm around the pitcher of kwagua juice and clinked it against Sheni and Gecki's mugs in celebration. Alan continued to grab trash off the beach, totally oblivious. Sheni grinned and shook his head.

A salvage company. Who'd have thought? But yeah, it was freakin' *perfect*.

Who else was better suited to finding diamonds in the rough?

THANK YOU FOR READING!

The adventure continues in Shadows in the Salvage.

And you might want to check out The Final Dawn if you haven't already – it's the series in which Sheni and the crew of the *Silver Hart* made their first ever appearance.

Turn the page for a full list of titles set in the same universe as Shadows in the Stone.

BOOKS IN THE "DARK STAR PANORAMA" UNIVERSE

Final Dawn Series

- The Final Dawn
- Thief of Stars
- A Dark Horizon
- The New World
- The Tin Soldiers
- Ghost of the Father
- The Stellar Abyss
- The Edge of Night
- The Fatal Dark

War for New Terra Series

- Sigma
- Iron Nest
- Royal Blood

Shadows in the Stars Series

- Shadows in the Stars
- Shadows in the Snow
- Shadows in the Stone
- Shadows in the Sands
- Shadows in the Salvage
- Shadows in the Storm

Kapamentis Crime Series

- A Cut Below
- Cut to the Bone
- Cut and Shut
- The Final Cut

Standalone Novels

- Saturnalia

SELECT NON-DSP TITLES

- Checking Out (Box Set)
- Blackwater (Box Set)
- The Portrait Lingers Like a Whisper
- Gerald Oddman

WANT A FREE, EXCLUSIVE BOOK?

Building a relationship with my readers is one of the best things about writing. Every now and then I send out newsletters with details on new releases, special offers and other bits of news relating to my books.

And if you sign up to the mailing list I'll even send you a **FREE** copy of *The Ultimate Dark Star Panorama Compendium*, an exclusive guide covering every aspect of my Dark Star Panorama universe, from a full timeline to a comprehensive encyclopaedia. It also contains *Before the Dawn*, a short prequel to my *Final Dawn* series.

Sign up today at twmashford.com.

ENJOY THIS BOOK? YOU CAN MAKE A BIG DIFFERENCE.

Reviews are the most powerful tool in my arsenal when it comes to getting attention for my books. As an indie author, I don't have quite the same financial muscle as a New York publisher. But what I *do* have is something even more effective:

A committed and loyal bunch of readers.

Honest reviews of my books help bring them to the attention of other readers.

If you've enjoyed this book I would be very grateful if you could spend just five minutes leaving a review (it can be as short as you like) on the book's Amazon page.

Thank you very much.

ABOUT THE AUTHOR

Tom Ashford lives just outside London, England with his wife Jenny and extremely needy cat, Kathleen.

An avid movie buff and video game addict, Tom loves all things science fiction. That's why he started the *Dark Star Panorama* universe – an ever-growing tapestry of epic space-faring stories including the *Final Dawn, Kapamentis Crime* and *War for New Terra* series.

His favourite authors are Terry Pratchett and Stephen King.

facebook.com/TWMAshford

instagram.com/ashfordtom

Printed in Dunstable, United Kingdom